DATE DUE

Apr 1, 2004			
4-15-04			
12/05			
2+18			
3/23/06			
2+20			
			PRINTED IN U.S.A
GAYLORD			

ON WINGS OF A
DRAGON

BY CORA TAYLOR

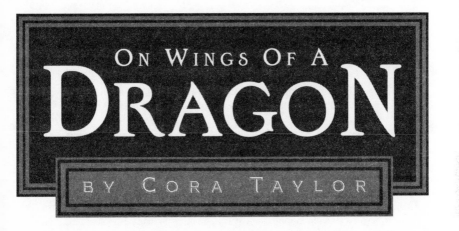

ON WINGS OF A
DRAGON

BY CORA TAYLOR

Fitzhenry & Whiteside

Copyright © 2001 by Cora Taylor

Published in Canada by Fitzhenry & Whiteside,
195 Allstate Parkway, Markham, Ontario L3R 4T8

Published in the United States by Fitzhenry & Whiteside,
121 Harvard Avenue, Suite 2, Allston, Massachusetts 02134

Fitzhenry & Whiteside acknowledges with thanks the Canada Council for the Arts, the
Government of Canada through the Book Publishing Industry Development Program
(BPIDP), and the Ontario Arts Council for their support of our publishing program.

Design by Wycliffe Smith

10 9 8 7 6 5 4 3 2 1

National Library of Canada Cataloguing in Publication Data

Taylor, Cora, 1936-
On wings of a dragon

ISBN 1-55041-674-X

I. Title.

PS8589.A88305 2001   jC813'.54   C2001-901080-X
                          PZ7.T21235On 2001

U.S. Cataloging-in-Publication Data
(Library of Congress Standards)

Taylor, Cora.
On wings of a dragon / by Cora Taylor. — 1st ed.
[256] p. ; cm.
Summary: Protected by her dragon companion, a young woman is sent
on a dangerous mission to restore the kingdom to its rightful heir.
ISBN: 1-55041-674-X
1. Fantasy. 2. Dragons — Fiction. I. Title.
[F] 21 2001 AC CIP

Acknowledgements

I'd like to express my gratitude to the Alberta Foundation for the Arts for a portion of the funding to travel to Tasmania, Australia for the position at Jane Franklin College, University of Hobart, where the work on this book began.

A big thanks to my daughter Wendy Mogg for making my map idea look like a map! And to Martin Springett for the wonderful cover art.

Thank you to all the people who read the manuscript and made suggestions: Janice MacDonald, Madeleine Mant, Sam Thomas, Eleanor McEachern and Peter Carver. Thanks to Suzanne Harris for her help with the names. Thanks to my editor Laura Peetoom for all the great suggestions and assistance with the final draft.

And a very special thank you to Earl Georgas for his love and support as I finished this book.

PART ONE

CHAPTER ONE

———·—·———

For three days it had rained, warm misty rain that smelled of trees she had once known in a place she could no longer remember. Kour'el stood on tiptoe reaching her cupped hand out of the window, holding it there, until her palm was wet. Then she brought her hand in to breathe and wash her face in the moisture so that the smell would linger and comfort her a little longer.

She didn't need to do that. Each morning an old woman with gnarled hands brought fresh water, placed it on the plain wooden stand that was the only piece of furniture in the small room, dropped Kour'el a courtesy and left without a word. She would have liked to see the old woman's face but it was always hidden by the thick folds of the hooded cloak that covered her face and swathed her body to shapelessness. Only the hands indicated that the person inside was old — and a woman.

The air smelled of the season before the cold time, too, but different somehow from what she was used to in her country. And how she had come here she was not sure. A long journey — parts of it so painful she could not remember. She remembered she had not been alone at first. She was sure she had not been alone at first. Yet it was so blurred, so dark and distant that she could not fathom who or what had been with her. And for the last part, the terrible part — then she had been all alone.

She waited. On days when the sun shone she could tell when it was morning. Once just after the old woman left, Kour'el had made a mark where the light fell, scratching with the shallow stone basin on the wall. After a few days of watching she knew that the old woman came each day at precisely the same time.

Knowing that — knowing that one small thing made Kour'el feel better. Somehow it lessened the despair and made her feel a strength she had not felt since she'd come here. She did not know when she'd come or how she'd got to this place. One day she had awakened lying on the straw pallet on the stone floor in this room. Awakened and slept again — for days it seemed.

She remembered falling — falling and fear and terrible pain — her back wrenching as if torn apart. Sometimes she would dream it again, except in her dreams she would begin the terrifying fall and then would catch herself in the air and swoop and soar and glide like the great condors at home. There! She'd remembered something of home. The condors' flight. And the smell of trees. It was a beginning. And a beginning was better than an ending any time.

CHAPTER TWO

The cat was coppery-black and hungry looking. It lived by its wits and moved in that independent way all cats have, and warily for it trusted no one. On the right hind leg a distinctive patch of white hair showed, the relic of a scar from some long ago battle.

Bron's chubby legs followed it unsteadily down the path. His sister Maighdlin glanced up from weaving a flower crown and frowned. She knew it was useless to call him back. Not while the cat walked in that slow, proud, tantalizing way just ahead of him, as if deliberately luring him away. She sighed and got to her feet, spilling the crimson and blue flowers everywhere. It was lovely to have a chance to sit in the sun here on the hillside instead of in the dark cottage spinning skein after skein of wool. But looking after the young one could be work too. If she was lucky, perhaps soon he would let the sunshine and the drowsy warmth of the day lull him to sleep and she could get some rest as well. She followed cat and child noiselessly down the path. There was no need to hurry — soon the cat would come to the wall of stones and have to turn, angling away along the wall and then she would simply scoop up her protesting brother and carry him away. She would tell him a story — he loved stories — until he fell asleep.

The cat came to the wall and paused as if to allow the

child to catch up. Bron was within inches now, laughing and reaching out chubby fingers to touch it. And Maighdlin gasped. It had not occurred to her the cat would jump — could jump. The wall was very high. But suddenly, in that soundless effortless way of cats, it leapt, feet touching a large dark stone partway up — boosting itself in one smooth motion. It sat for a moment at the top of the wall and then dropped from sight on the other side.

Maighdlin waited for the cry of protest from the baby — knowing she was close enough to pick him up and comfort him and knowing he did not know she was, for she had been silent in her following. He didn't cry at all but ran to slap his hands angrily against the wall as if to punish it for thwarting him and making the cat disappear.

"That will hurt, small one...." she began and once again was amazed. A small portion of the stone wall swung away, like a gate, smoothly and noiselessly. Maighdlin stared. As far as she knew there had not been a gate. The wall had been here as long as she could remember. Perhaps she had not noticed this place in the wall. Who would? The stones fit so smoothly that there was no sign of any break in them unless — unless someone, even someone not very strong, pushed against it. Maighdlin darted after her brother.

Bron had fallen not far from the gate and as she bent to pick him up something nudged her. She turned and saw the gate was closing again — smoothly and noiselessly just as it had opened. She scooped her brother up and spun back through the gate as it seemed to gather momentum and slam angrily behind her.

She stood trembling, hugging the little boy to her, rocking him to console him although strangely enough he was not crying, had not uttered a sound. Still she held him tight, for her own consolation, her own comfort. There had been something relentless about the gate and it had unnerved her more than the strange sight she had seen on the other side.

Maighdlin turned and walked steadily across the slope of the hill to where she had been sitting. Settled once more amongst the wilting flowers she had picked earlier she stared back at the wall intently — as if she could see within. She still held the child and sang softly, unconsciously. It was an old song her grandmother had taught her when Maighdlin was as young as Bron was now. It must have been then, for her grandmother had died so very long ago Maighdlin could scarcely remember her. She remembered only the sharp smell of fresh buttermilk in the churn, the feel of soft wrinkled skin against her cheek and this song. And only a little of the melody and a word or two of that remained in her memory. "...shule, shule, shule..." she sang and the child in her arms was still and quiet.

So quiet she looked down to see if he was asleep. No. He held something in his hand and was touching it gently with his finger. A butterfly? She wondered. He was always chasing them — had he managed to catch one at last? Did she see a movement where something glistened between his fingers?

"What have you there? Open your hand and show Maudie." She coaxed as she gently pried his chubby fingers open one by one.

She was careful. She knew if she upset him he'd throw it or squeeze tighter — his tantrums were unpredictable. "The flower opens petal by petal..." she sang, using an old finger play song all babies in her land learned to love. It worked. Soon his fist was open and there on the palm of his hand lay something so delicate and fragile she was afraid to touch it. Silver and spider-web thin, it looked brittle as spun glass. How had it survived inside that grubby little fist for even a moment? She poked it gently, tentatively with her finger and realized it was not glass at all. It bent to her touch, soft as thistledown. It was no butterfly unless it was part of a wing, but no creature she had ever seen, even the rarest of the forest moths that hid their trembling wings from the sun, were like this. There was a warmth too that wrapped itself around her finger. She had never felt anything like it.

She forgot the mysterious gate, the cat, the crown of flowers she had almost finished. Rising awkwardly, still holding her brother in her arms, she ran to the only person who might be able to tell her what it was. The person in the land she most trusted.

Chapter Three

Gradually Kour'el's strength had come back. Each day the old woman left not only the ewer of water but a pitcher of broth as well. The broth had been thin at first when she was so weak she could not move from the pallet. Then, even though the woman placed it on the floor beside her, Kour'el did not have the strength to lift the heavy pitcher but could only tilt it to take sips. Lately the broth was thicker and there were vegetables that Kour'el could not identify — flavorless, colorless stringy things that stuck in her teeth. There were chunks of meat too, tender and tasting sweet with a faint savor of charring. Kour'el drank it all, fished every last scrap of meat and bit of vegetable out of the pitcher. Her strength seemed to come back more quickly then, but even before she was strong enough to stand she had begun to plan.

First she had quietly studied every inch of the stone walls and floor of the cell so that even before she attempted to walk she knew the spacing of each block in the walls and could anticipate each bump and crack as she made her first painful steps across the floor. She would walk until nausea or lightheadedness drove her back to lie down. It took her the whole day to make her way to the wooden stand opposite her pallet, circling the room in order to hold onto the wall as she moved. That was the day she learned something she hadn't been aware of before. She had truly *circled* the room. Why had she not noticed it was *round* as she had studied the walls from where she was? Perhaps it was a trick of the light that entered from the window above her as she lay. Perhaps the room was not truly round but only curved.

There was no doubt that the room had its secrets somewhere in the walls because the next morning the old woman did not place things on the floor by the bed but set them on the table as if she somehow knew Kour'el was able to get up and around at last. And so it was Kour'el knew someone was watching her and she became circumspect in her examination of the room: pretending to walk for exercise she studied the stone walls that surrounded her; lying on her pallet seemingly staring into space she studied the domed ceiling above. But try as she might she could find no peephole through which someone might be watching.

She *was* more careful though. To the mark on the wall added a circle and put crude moon shapes within it; then she knelt before it as though it were holy, in the hope that the Watcher might not realize it was her timepiece.

On days there was no sun her rough sundial would not work and without it she had no way of knowing whether it was morning or afternoon. Without the sun she often slept too long and then was awake in the cold night darkness — listening. She seldom heard anything but the wind. Few sounds came to her window. She must be far from everyone, she thought. Just herself and the old woman in some stone cottage in some deep forest. No, not in the forest. Surely she would have heard the songs of birds, the rustle of leaves, the creak of branches in the wind if there were woods nearby.

She jumped when the heavy wooden door swung noise-lessly open and the old woman entered. Kour'el had tried listening for footsteps coming down the hall but the woman's shoes were made of heavy fleece and made no sound. She stood watching as the woman left today's water and soup and picked up the jugs from yesterday. Then she did something new. She reached under her cloak and brought out a large brown loaf of bread, placed it on the table, dropped a stiff curtsy and left, the door closing silent-ly behind her. No sound to indicate whether she walked down a hall, down stairs or stood outside, listening....

Kour'el did not care. There was no knife so she tore chunks of bread from the loaf. The bread was heavy and held lumps of hard grain that jarred her teeth. She picked them out and ate more carefully. It tasted stale and was gritty as if bits of the grindstone had been baked with the flour. Kour'el's tongue rebelled at the coarse bitter flavor of it but she knew that she needed whatever nutrients it con-tained, and it would help satisfy the hunger that never quite went away as she got stronger and took more exer-cise. She ate only a portion before she picked up the pitch-er with the broth and began to drink. She drained it, for she had learned that if left very long a thick greasy scum formed that stuck in her throat and made her gag. She would save the vegetables, most of the meat and the rest of the bread to eat later. Eagerly, for it was the only part she really wanted, she ate two pieces of the strange-tasting meat. She left the rest reluctantly. But she felt better as though transfused with strength from her simple meal.

And now there was no hiding what she was about to do from anyone watching. Today was the first day she'd felt strong enough to do it. She set the heavy dishes on the floor and picked up the wooden stand to carry it to the window high above the head of her pallet. The stand was heavier than she thought. Her back began to ache and the stand bumped against her shins painfully so that finally she dragged it the rest of the way. She realized she was still weak. She was sure that she could at one time have climbed up without trouble. Now she hauled herself up slowly, gripping the iron window bars with both hands. For something that seemed so heavy and solid the stand wobbled and Kour'el was glad that she had the bars to hold.

It had been raining again but it had stopped and when she looked out streaks of sunlight broke through the clouds. She was not sure what she had been expecting when she looked down but it was not what she saw.

Far below her there was a lake, its surface unruffled by waves. It was as flat as a picture but the water gleamed copper as if fired from within. Beyond it stretched a barren brown hillside. Desolate. No trees, no cottages, no people, nothing but the strange sandy brown hill, and she could not see the near shore. She pressed her face against the bars, but the stone wall was so thick that, for all she could see, she was on a strange island.

She moved her hands to other bars, as if changing her viewpoint, and in this way tested — without seeming to — each of the bars. They were solid. She had expected nothing less. Escape would never be possible through this window, even if she knew how far the drop beneath it was or whether the landing would be on land or rocks or the lake. Involuntarily she drew a deep breath, then stifled a sob. She would not let the Watcher know she despaired.

But the indrawn breath reminded her again of the sharp, wild scent of trees. She had seen no trees and she climbed down just as puzzled as before.

She left the stand where it was and laid stiffly down on the pallet. She would rest and then move it back when she felt stronger. And she could look forward to the pieces of meat she had saved.

She did not mean to sleep but she did. This time she slept without dreaming.

CHAPTER FOUR

Maighdlin was completely out of breath by the time she came to the old man's hut. As always when the day was fine, he sat on the heavy wooden bench just outside the door, nodding in the warmth of the sun. On very hot days he moved to another bench on the other side of the door where the lazuli bush with its bright blue flowers shaded him from the sun.

It took Maighdlin awhile to get breath enough to speak and the old man sat still as death. He had often frightened her with the intensity of his sleeping, his lack of movement or signs of life. She'd grown used to it now. "Old One," she gasped, "GranDa...."

She waited for him to start to life, for his faded blue eyes to open and focus on her. Then there would be the slow happy smile that would spread over his wrinkled face, starting it seemed somewhere deep in his beard and ending in the shaggy hair that hung like a fringe around his head. She waited for him to speak; it gave her even more time to catch her breath. She sat down at his feet where the old man could see her best, but she did not let go of Bron and the treasure he still clutched in his hand even though he wriggled to get away.

"There you are, my Galea," he said at last. The smile, and the special name he used for her and her alone, warmed her as she had known it would. Now she must wait for the usual questions: "Where have you been?" "What have you seen?"

Grandfather said she was his eyes and his legs now that he was a prisoner of legs that would not go very far and eyes that could not see very well.

He reached down, chucked the struggling baby under each of his chins, then ran a gnarled finger down the softness of her cheek.

"Where have you been, my Galea? What have you seen?"

"Grandfather!" Maighdlin tried to curb her eagerness. She would begin with the wall, for surely Bron had found the wonderful thing when he'd fallen down just inside. It must have been what kept him from crying. She could see that his chubby knees were scratched and bleeding so he must have hurt himself but been distracted by what he had found.

"GranDa..." she paused deliberately. "I've been on the hillside by the stone wall. GranDa, how long has that wall been there and how did it come to be?"

"Grandchild," he smiled teasingly, "why do you always answer a question with a question?"

Maighdlin laughed and with the laugh relaxed a little. Even Bron decided to sit still a minute and laugh as if he understood the joke. "Because, Wise One," Maighdlin smiled up at him, sharing their game, "how else will I ever learn anything?" She waited now.

"The wall," said the old man, his face serious with remembering, "is as old as you. Twice seven years it's been there. Twice seven years since the woe came on the land and our king was lost to us."

Maighdlin shivered as she always did when her grandfather talked of the time of woe. Even though she knew King Vassill still lived, no one saw him now except on special occasions and then only from a great distance as the queen guided his stumbling steps to the palace balcony. His picture still showed on the laws and proclamations and his name was still signed beneath, but in her whole life she had heard of no one who'd had an audience with him. He spoke only to the queen and the princesses. She knew that to her grandfather, who had been the king's favorite huntsman and companion in the fields and forests, King Vassill might as well have perished. The old man mourned him still. Both men had been injured one terrible day and the king had lain for months near death while the land had weakened without him.

"I tried to see him when I could walk a little again...." He shook his head. "She had them turn me away. She said he could see no one, not even his old friend." His head hung sorrowfully. Then he looked at Maighdlin without seeing her. "A man needs a friend," he said simply and then, softly as if to himself, "...even if he is married to the most beautiful woman in the world." He sighed. "But then she was angry and blamed me for the accident. I think she blamed him too, but in a different way, as if our being there that day had been a betrayal."

Maighdlin knew her grandfather would soon be enveloped in this ancient silent sorrow. She could hold her news no longer. And she wanted to know, to show him the treasure Bron had found.

"But *I have seen* something and *I have been* somewhere, GranDa!" The words tumbled out. "Did you know there is a gate...a piece of the wall that opens? Do you know what is on the other side?"

The old man started and for a moment his attention focused on her face with a much younger man's intensity. She realized that he was not as old as he seemed; or perhaps she suddenly saw an echo of the man her grandfather had been before the accident.

His voice when he spoke was sharper, younger too. "You have seen the tower?" he asked as his watery blue eyes searched her face.

It was Maighdlin's turn to be startled and stare at him. The wall was so high and it circled the hilltop. When had he seen it? She knew the children believed the wall had been built to keep them from falling from a steep cliff on the other side of the hill. No one, in all their years of imaginary play and listening to grown-up gossip, had mentioned a tower.

He didn't wait for an answer. "How did you get in?" and then his concern showed even stronger — "How did you get *out*?"

"Bron pushed the wall and...and it opened...and I went after him...and he'd fallen and when I picked him up, the gate was closing and I jumped back. I only just glimpsed the tower as the gate closed."

Her seeing had been so brief, so caught up in the fear she had felt at the moment, she might not have understood what it was had her grandfather not mentioned it. Now she could remember it — the cold dark look of its stones — the roof a strange metallic color that seemed to swallow the sunlight.

There was true concern in her grandfather's face as he looked at the baby in her arms. "It is a miracle that you were close enough and quick enough to save him...to save you both."

Maighdlin looked down at her little brother. She'd hardly noticed that he wasn't struggling to be free any more. He had slumped against her, sound asleep, his fist still curled tightly around the treasure he had found.

"The tower..." he began more calmly now. "The tower...has been there forever." He frowned. "At least it was there in my grandfather's day and his grandfather before him." His voice sank to a whisper. Maighdlin was amazed to see him look around suspiciously as if they might not be alone.

"But it was considered an evil place...a place of darkness...though I never heard of anyone...good or *evil* being there...or any *thing*, other than harmless empty stones. Still, as far as memory goes people were afraid to go there and no one talked of it."

"But you weren't afraid, GranDa?" Maighdlin felt herself being drawn into the mystery.

That cheered him and he laughed softly, smiling down at her. "No, child...and even less afraid was the king! Now there was a man who knew no fear."

As always when he spoke of King Vassill before the accident the old man's voice was young and proud. But Maighdlin knew that this talk could only lead to more despair as her grandfather remembered the accident that had changed everything. Not that he would talk of it. He had never told her any details of that night — when she asked questions he shut her out. Now he had fallen into a brooding silence and she knew she must distract him. What better than the puzzle that had brought her here in the first place?

She had been gently prying open the baby's fingers as her grandfather spoke and now the amazing object sparkled and shimmered in the sunlight, moving gently in the breeze but clinging to the chubby palm. She did not dare remove it but stood instead holding the sleeping child's hand out to the old man.

"And what is this, Wise One? The little one found it inside the wall."

CHAPTER FIVE

Kour'el had not meant to break the pitcher. It slipped out of her fingers as she was returning it to the stand and it shattered into dozens of shards at her feet. Now she stared at the pieces of meat and realized that she could not eat them. The fragments were too sharp and too mixed up with the food. For the first time in her imprisonment a wave of despair threatened to engulf her. She fought it back.

Her craving for the meat she had so carefully saved amazed her and she turned and went to lie down, shutting her eyes to hold back the tears.

This was ridiculous! She had gone without food before. Why, once when she was traveling with... She stopped. The name eluded her, slipped fishlike from her grasp but she had *almost* remembered something. A trip, a name... something from the past. Almost.

She lay there, feeling weak and hopeless. The craving for food, for the wasted meat should not be so strong, her disappointment so devastating. But she had waited so long, until the light began to fade, saving the last food so that she might sleep the night without rumblings of hunger. She'd been holding back so that she might enjoy the wonderful sensation of comfort she always seemed to get from eating, so that it would nourish her sleep and she would not toss hungrily, half-awake in the cold darkness.

Now she dreaded the night. She lay gazing at the way the last rays of light seemed to sweep the walls before twilight.

A wave of nausea and weakness swept over her. She knew the food, particularly the meat, was strengthening but this was more than that. And it frightened her. As always her response to fear was to lie very still like some small forest animal when its mother calls the danger warning. Where had she learned this? It had been with her for a long time. And she knew even very large creatures could do it, for people can be blind to things that blend into their surroundings.

Thinking about these things eased her tension; gradually her muscles relaxed, her breathing slowed. She slept.

She was hiding. Stretched along the branch of a dane-tree in the forest, she was hiding in the open, in plain view. And men were walking down the path toward her. Hunters or soldiers, their clothes glistened in the dappling sunlight that reached through the high branches to the forest floor. She was afraid. And still as a stone.

She was tired and weak and she was waiting for her friend to come back. It had been a very long time. The soldiers or hunters stopped and then to her horror began to make camp close by. Sometimes they moved almost directly beneath her, and then the sharp dark smell of their sweat drifted up to her, the smokiness of their leather clothing, the harsh smell of tobacco. Then another smell from the campfire — food — and she knew she would have to wait here without moving all night, unless she could slip away while they slept.

*So the night stretched ahead of her, hungry and un-
comfortable but more than that, full of worry. What if
her friend came back after the fire burned low and did
not see the camp until too late? What if he was seen?
But instinctively she knew she was the one the soldiers
pursued, the hunters hunted. So she waited, listening
through the nearby sounds of eating and belching and
rough laughter for a familiar sound, a creak of a branch,
his approach. Gradually she relaxed. The hunters were
making too much noise for anyone to accidentally
stumble upon them now. She closed her eyes and slept.*

Kour'el felt herself falling, woke with a start and clutched
for the branch. But there was no branch — no forest, only
the straw pallet, the stones around her. She lay there letting her eyes get used to the dark room until the darkness
assumed shapes. She remembered the dream clearly and it
gave her hope. Perhaps she would remember that she had
been pursued, and then by whom — and then why. And
then perhaps she would know how she had come to be here
in this strangely shaped room.

She rose stiffly. On the opposite side of the room from
the door a tiny bow of stones formed a bulge in the tower.
A seat, with an iron grating over the dark hole. She hadn't
used this at first — there'd been a bucket for her to relieve
herself but now that she could scramble up and walk to
this, the bucket had been taken away. She could see nothing through the grating — nothing but blackness, no matter how bright the day.

She jabbed her toe on one of the shards on her way
back. Her cry of surprise filled the room and seemed to
echo in the stone walls. The sound of her own voice

shocked her. She'd forgotten how loud she could be and then the sound was probably magnified by the stones. Surely she would be heard. Then she thought that perhaps, she might benefit from the broken pitcher after all. There were so many pieces, so scattered of such diverse sizes, that a few would not be missed when the old woman gathered them up. She kicked some across the floor in the dark toward her pallet, shuffling as if trying to feel her way.

She lay quietly for a long time before she began to reach her hand out, throwing it as if tossing in her sleep, then rolling over and gradually, in what she hoped seemed like the normal movements of sleep, tucking the shards under the pallet. She doubted that anything could be seen in that darkness but she was determined not to risk it. Luckily the pallet cover was sewn in a loose running stitch and, by lying on her stomach with her hands tucked underneath as if making a pillow for her head, she could loosen an opening big enough to slip the sharp stone inside and then pull the thread so that it would not show to a casual glance.

It was just one more thing that gave her confidence although she could not at present think of any way in which these shards would help her. What helped her now was knowing she had something. Something that was hers alone. A secret.

She fell asleep then and wakened in the pre-dawn dark, sweating and fearful. This dream had not been clear or told her anything as the other one had. This was the familiar terror. The falling, the fire, the terrible burning smell and a scream that seemed to come from her own throat but was bigger than anything human. And then the back-wrenching agony of pain and then nothing, but this room and her aching body.

CHAPTER SIX

———•———

Petaurus saw the disappointment in his granddaughter's eyes as he shook his head. He reached out and touched the delicate silvery material nestling on the baby's palm.

"Of course," he said, "my eyes are not what they were."

The old man hated misleading Maighdlin but he loved her dearly and feared what would happen if even a whisper of rumor spread from something she said. Something might reach the wrong ears and cause... he did not even know what it might cause but he remembered the queen's men questioning him after the accident. Who or what had attacked them? An enemy? A fierce beast? What had they been hunting? What had caused their terrible injuries?

Even then, barely conscious and in great pain, he had protected King Vassill and kept his word. For the king had not lost consciousness immediately after the attack and had told him what to say. Told him to keep the secret of that day — and the promised meeting by the tower. Eventually his inquisitors had grown tired of hearing the same response day after day and had left him alone.

So he clung once again to his old loyalty to the king even though this time it cost him much more dearly. It hurt to see her expectation in him dimming like this. These days she was the only one who respected him, and in his whole life, the only one who had thought him wise. But it was the best way.

He had to think about this. Everything was coming too fast. His brain had slowed with his body and he had never, despite his granddaughter naming him Wise One, been more than a humble huntsman and devoted follower of the king. His king had led and he had followed. The king had thought they could do something and Petaurus had made it possible, for he had been clever with his hands in those days and had the strength to do anything his king wished. Now to the child he was the Wise One simply because he had lived long and knew how things had been in the joyous days when King Vassill ruled, well and strong. And because he remembered when the land had been happy.

And now today, so much was happening. The wall had moved. The tower had been seen, though only briefly. And this...this strange and wonderful thing had come to light. Best yet it had been found by an innocent child. He hesitated yet could not resist. He reached out and touched the delicate silvery material nestling on the baby's palm.

Soft and light and warm as a spring breeze it caressed his finger. And with the touch he remembered. Everything came back.

Once he had been wrapped in it. Swaddled in it like a baby and held from falling. Clinging to the edge of the cliff beneath the tower on a night with no moon while the king strove to save him from falling further — and then it had been the king who fell. The king who was so hurt that when Petaurus had reached him, dragging himself down the narrow ledge trail, he'd thought his lord was dead, his face shone so white in the darkness. Like a ghost — a will-o'-the-wisp in the shadows.

Then, all that had been important was saving his king. Their purpose for going there no longer mattered to him though later, when the queen's inquisitors were gone, he had done what he could, then waited in vain for word from the king.

"What is it, GranDa?" Maighdlin said eagerly. "You look as if you've remembered something."

Petaurus chided himself. The maiden was so sharp-eyed she missed little. The queen's men had been much easier to mislead. He shook his head sadly.

"No." He fumbled in his pocket as if looking for his pipe — he was buying time to think of an answer to satisfy her curiosity. "I only marvel at the world, which holds such lovely things that we can never see them all, no matter how old..." he laughed teasingly, "...or how wise we become."

Her face fell with disappointment but she smiled through it understandingly and he was grateful for that.

But there was more than just the magical material to worry about. He could not hide his concern about that and he would not try. "You're sure, my girl, that there was no one on the hillside? Even down on the village path...who might have seen the wall open? Someone who while they might not have seen you go in...might have been coming up the path and seen you coming out?"

His heart warmed to her once again. For unlike many, young or old, she did not answer immediately but thought about it, her face solemn with remembering. He knew she was putting herself back on the hillside reliving the moment she had flung herself out of the way of the wall that was moving shut behind her. He had noticed this before. She had a talent for reliving things and grasping details that might otherwise be missed. He knew that when she spoke she would be sure of what she had seen and it would be accurate in every way.

"No," she said finally. "There was no one on the path and further down the hill we would not have been visible...nor the wall that opened...for it curves there and does not show. But we sat then, the little one and I...until I saw what he held." She shook her head positively. "Nobody came in all that time...and we passed no one on our way to you...and we ran!" She finished triumphantly, confident of the truth she told him.

The relief he felt was strong, yet tempered with enough alarm that he could make his warning ring true. "You understand that you must tell no one what has happened," he said sternly. "Neither of the gate nor how it opened nor of your being inside or what you saw there. Nothing!"

She nodded and he knew he could trust her not to speak of it.

"I think, GranDa," she said nodding towards the child's hand, "that you should take that and put it somewhere safe...or..." Her voice faltered.

"It seems too wondrous to be lost," he mused, reading her thoughts. "A terrible waste to destroy something so amazing."

"Yes." She smiled up at him hopefully. "You could hide it somewhere."

He nodded. "And I will tell you where, so that...." He left the words unspoken. He knew she understood. Somewhere she could retrieve it when he was gone. And perhaps in some safer time she would learn what it was. He nodded. He would do it. He owed her that for her discretion and for his love for her.

She picked it gently from the baby's palm and handed it to her grandfather. Bron stirred and grieved as if his sleep was saddened by the loss, but he did not waken.

Maighdlin rose awkwardly trying not to disturb her sleeping brother. She leaned forward and kissed her grandfather gently and he stroked her long hair tenderly in return. It was all the farewell they needed.

He watched until she was out of sight and then stared for a few moments at the wonder in his hand. But there was no time to cherish it for he feared even the most casual passerby now, though there were few enough in his far corner of the village. He seized his cane and stood painfully, looking around furtively before he went into the hut. Once there he walked to the fireplace, removed a slab of stone from the hearth, and lifted out a small silver box.

When he had hidden it again he threw a few scraps of wood onto the coals then went over to the cot with its thick straw mattress and lay down. He lay there staring as the flames began, wild shapes and leaping visions. Dragon flames...a funeral pyre he'd stood by long ago.

He did not sleep. He lay a long time wondering how he could contact the king. He must contact the king.

Kour'el lay a long time feigning sleep. She did not want her Watcher to know she was distraught. Had she tossed and turned in her sleep? Moaned or spoken? If they could see her could they hear her too? She must assume they could. She must be on guard at all times, even when sleeping.

She welcomed the soft light of dawn that gradually changed the darkness into shadows, then shapes, until she could make out the familiar wooden stand across from her, the irregular colors of the stones that formed her walls. Now she could move, stretch and yawn, and feign awakening just as she had slumber. She raised herself on one elbow and surveyed the mess of broken pitcher across from her. There was no broom, nothing she could have tidied it with, she could only sit patiently on the pallet and wait for the old woman. The beam of sunlight that entered the room at sunrise had now begun its journey across the wall to the place that marked the time of the old woman's arrival.

Kour'el waited, legs wrapped together with the soles of her feet up. It was a position she sat in automatically, something that came naturally. She could even sleep so and now because she had awakened so early her head began to nod.

"You must do this..." Someone was speaking to her but it was dark and she could not see the face. The voice

was kind though. Familiar. It was a voice she trusted so she nodded. She would do whatever was asked; that was her training, that was what she had been waiting for.

"It may be too late to send anyone," the voice continued, "it has taken a very long time for the news to reach us. Normally we cannot go unless we are called but in this case we haven't heard from our messengers and our ways are blocked. Enough time has passed though that we must make contact even if we have not been called." Something shifted in the darkness behind the voice — a heavy scraping sound and then all was still except for a gentle rustling that was almost inaudible.

Kour'el waited, not daring to speak. This sounded important. Why had she been chosen over so many others, older and better-trained?

"We have chosen you because there are disturbances...one at either end of the zone. They could be natural...some of it is surely typhoons or quaking of the earth but to have them occurring at such distance at the same time...we must be on guard. There are rumors too...we are concerned for the vessel." The voice, even the rustling ceased and all was deathly still.

So, she was being sent because the others were needed elsewhere. And it was something that was most likely long since finished. Something that could not be overlooked, must be checked into — but what point wasting anyone experienced on it when there was little hope that anything could be done?

"There may be something...and we cannot let our friends perish...have perished without some effort being made."

The rustling began again. "But in case they are not there you will be given a name as you leave." The light flickered and went out before it could illumine the darkness.

Kour'el did not need that light. There was no mystery here, only out there — where she was being sent. Her first quest.

The light flickered again. "You will take Api'Naga." It was half question, half statement. And then a dazzling flash to let her know she need not answer — the choice was hers.

There was no choice. It was what she had been hoping for. Her companion during her training — her trainer almost. Api'Naga would save her time and strength if she could ride the long way. More than that, his wisdom and experience would mean that she had at least a chance of living to return, whether or not she succeeded.

Kour'el's head jerked up bumping painfully against the stone wall. Had she heard something? Was the old woman coming? But she heard no sound and the door did not open. She looked at the beam of sunlight. It had moved far beyond the mark when the woman usually came. The shards still littered the floor, there was no new pitcher, the old woman had not been here while she dozed and dreamed.

She was suddenly afraid. The daily arrival had been part of her life since she'd recovered her senses. Of all the fears and worries she'd had since she'd found herself a prisoner here, it had not occurred to her that she might be abandoned here to starve as if in some oubliette, forgotten by everyone. Who knew she was here beside the old woman?

What if the old woman had perished in some way without telling anyone of the girl she tended? Kour'el's fear pushed away all thought and memory. It was all she could do not to scream.

She tried to calm herself — most likely it was just that something had happened to make the woman late. And if she did not come today, she would surely come tomorrow. Perhaps this was punishment for breaking the jug. Whoever watched would have reported it. Kour'el realized that knowing she was watched, although making her secretive, had in some way kept her from being lonely. The feeling of constant prying eyes was awful but it kept her from the terrible feeling of isolation that swept over her now. This overwhelming fear would possess her and drive her mad if she let it.

It was some minutes as she settled herself again to wait before the dream came back to her. And for all her immediate worries it gave her strength. She had been on some mission — a quest to find out what had happened to someone. How long ago? She had known the trail was cold, she had known she was being sent because she was dispensable. But she had gone gladly with some bright optimism that she would succeed. It was not just youthful exuberance and thirst for adventure. She would not have had much hope had she been alone. But Api'Naga was with her. And she had faith in Api'Naga.

This time a tear did escape and she brushed it angrily away. It was not despair this time but frustration. She remembered the dream well. Well enough to know it was a memory of what had really happened. That she had stood listening in quiet darkness to her orders and that she had taken great comfort and strength from the knowledge that she would have such a worthy companion. Yes. She could relive it in all clarity — *that* was not the frustration. But she could not go beyond. The dream was like this room. She knew nothing outside it, nor beyond it. She did not know how she came to it, nor how she would depart. And apart from the comfort the name had given her and the confidence it instilled she could not — though she tried desperately — remember who Api'Naga was.

She got up to pace the edge of the room, walking carefully so as not to cut her feet if she stepped on a shard. A wave of weakness swept over her and she paused. Going without food for one day should not have made such a difference. Indeed she had probably eaten as much yesterday as she usually did since there had been the bread added to her usual food. Bread instead of meat, that was all — but still she almost staggered and fell. She turned and walked slowly back to the pallet. She must conserve her strength in case...in case the old woman did not come again tomorrow. She pushed the thought away. She would not think of it. She would rest and then she would go and have a few sips of the water that she knew was left.

She usually waited until it was almost time for the old woman to arrive and then she would use the last of the water to wash her face and clean herself. Today because she had slept she had not done so. That was something to be thankful for. She did not know how long that water would last and thirst was a far greater danger than hunger.

She concentrated on the dream again. It was like having one piece to a puzzle and no overall picture. Even worse than that, no other pieces to fit to it.

Except that she did! There was that other little dream of hiding in the tree from the soldiers and worrying about someone returning and being seen. That would be Api'Naga of course! The two pieces were far apart in the puzzle but the one added to the other. They had come on the quest and somehow were being pursued by those hunters or soldiers. And they had been separated. Had they got back together before — before the awful ending that she could not remember? Or had she still been alone then?

Two pieces of a puzzle. It seemed hopeless and yet two days ago she had nothing. Nothing but the scent of trees and a feeling of flying. Oh yes — and the faint memory of condors or something else high in the sky above her.

CHAPTER EIGHT

Maighdlin walked slowly back to the village singing softly to her brother. "The vessel will come and the land will be free..." She wondered what had put the song in her head. It was old and once had been most popular. She remembered that from when she was little. It had been a song of hope. Now the people seldom sang and the idea of freedom seemed hopeless. Once, when she had sung it to GranDa he had given her a strange look, then spoke sadly. "It is too late, I fear." Now she sang it only as a lullaby to Bron. He had not wakened when she'd left the hut but she liked to sing to him, liked his sleepy head on her shoulder, although her arms were beginning to ache from his weight.

She heard the noise before she saw the soldiers. The sound of someone shouting, the low murmuring rumble a crowd makes when confused and upset. She rounded the bend in the path leading to the village and stopped to watch. The crowd was quieting now, focusing their attention on the captain who had climbed the stone steps in front of the square where the people were. She scanned the crowd and saw her mother and all the other women, glancing around too, grouped together faces anxious.

She remembered this happening before. When she was much younger, the soldiers had come and taken many of the young men from the village to train for war. None had come back. But why was her mother concerned? Bron was much too little — she had no one to worry about.

"This is the second reading of the proclamation of Her Majesty the Queen Mariah," the captain began in a loud voice.

Strange, thought Maighdlin, why not *his* Majesty King Vassill? So the shouting before had been the first reading. She glanced around the crowd again. Near the back she glimpsed her friend Mala. Maighdlin tried to catch her eye but Mala was shrinking back, slipping quietly away. Gunn the blacksmith had stepped in front of her hiding her with his bulk and when he moved again Mala was gone, though Maighdlin thought she saw a flash of her vibrant red hair further back in the crowd. What was she doing? She looked around but could see none of her friends, no girls her own age. Were they all hidden in the crowd? The ring of soldiers at the back would surely prevent anyone going very far.

"Know that all maidens of twelve to fifteen summers are required to leave now to perform service at the palace for Her Majesty. Those who do not come immediately will be hunted down and imprisoned." He paused. From where he stood he could see what was going on in the crowd as well as Maighdlin could. "This is the second reading."

Maighdlin began to back away. Slowly. Perhaps if she did not move too quickly there was still time to slip around the bend in the road and run back to GranDa's hut. He would know where she could hide. He knew many things. She inched backwards, praying that the child in her arms would not pick this time to waken and cry.

Things were happening in the crowded square below. Two younger girls were being dragged forward by soldiers. One was the butcher's daughter, who'd put on airs because their family always had plenty to eat while others sometimes had to make meals of tubers dug from the hillside when their gardens failed and they had nothing to trade for meat. It would go hard on her being a serving maid. Harder still these days for life was not easy and rumor had it food was scarce even at the palace since the time of woe.

She continued to inch her way back as the captain announced the third reading of proclamation. She could no longer see much of the square. Soon she'd be totally cut off in the turn of the path and if she could not see the soldiers, they would not see her and she would be safe. At least safe for a little while to run and find a hiding place.

She realized that she had been holding her breath and let it go softly. Her arms ached from the heavy baby but she was careful not to shift position even slightly. He must not waken. Not now. There was screaming now as one of the soldiers dragged a girl forward, her bright hair snapping sparks in the sunlight. Mala! She was so vain about her hair and now it had been a flash of it moving through the crowd that alerted one of the soldiers.

Poor Mala! She was taken — that made it real and ugly and true. Maighdlin stopped and stood as if turned to stone.

Perhaps if she had kept moving her mother might not have looked up and seen her and the soldier facing *her* might not have seen the changed expression and turned to see what caught the woman's gaze.

He began to run and Maighdlin knew it was too late. Even had she been able to drop her brother she could not out-distance the soldiers now running behind him, could not run to GranDa, bringing the wrath of the soldiers on him when he tried to defend her. He would do that, Maighdlin knew. And what would these men care for the life of an old man who could not walk very well — even though he had once been a companion of the king?

Maighdlin took a deep breath and began to walk with all the dignity she could manage. Walking as befit the granddaughter of a proud good man — straight down the path toward the crowd and the captain. The young soldier closest to her stopped and let her walk by without touching her, only falling into step a little behind and to the side as she passed. The other two stopped running and turned back to the crowd.

There was a fight now. Young Brede, trying to wrest his betrothed, Marika, away from a soldier, had struggled and been slashed by a sword and was being carried away bleeding while Marika's screams tore the air as she fought against the soldier. It took two of them to drag her away. Maighdlin's heart was sorriest for her. Marika would have been sixteen when the moon waned again and they would have been wed and as a married woman she would be exempt from palace service.

She was aware of the young soldier beside her as she crossed the open part of the square in front of the captain. She could not see his face but she sensed his nearness. She wondered if he would try to grab her arm when she passed the place where the girls were being herded and held, but he did not. It was as if he knew why she crossed the square to the woman in the crowd facing her.

She said nothing as she placed her still-sleeping brother in their mother's arms. Their eyes met and Maighdlin caught the look of pain and remorse in her mother's eyes. She only shook her head, patted the older woman's shoulder and turned back, almost brushing against the young man at her side. Still he did not push her towards the other girls but held back and let her walk to stand with the others. Mala ran to her and clung, her face already mottled with weeping.

CHAPTER NINE

The day dragged on. The sunlight was now slanting and would soon no longer shine in the window and still the old woman had not come. Once Kour'el had thought she heard something — a moan from somewhere but though she listened until it seemed her head would break the sound did not come again. Perhaps it had been the wind. She hoped it had been the wind.

She was tempted to look out of the window. But she feared she did not have the strength to drag the stand across the floor, to pull herself up on top of it. She felt weakened, drained of all energy and will. And hungry — ravenously, desperately hungry. She had even gone to search among the scraps of pitcher for the pieces of meat she knew must still be there. Walking slowly across the room holding the walls for support, she had found that although the bits of stringy vegetable were still there, there was no trace of the meat. Had she dreamed it? No, she was sure she'd left some. She remembered seeing the pieces caught in the jagged edges of the broken pitcher. Now they were gone. As if they had melted away in the night.

She had almost crawled back to the pallet. All she wanted was to rest. Not to think at all. She curled up on her side, closed her eyes and slept.

There was wind in her face and stars above her.

Strange stars in patterns she had never seen before. What world was this they had traveled to? She could feel the strong body beneath her effortlessly gliding and soaring. hour after hour. Api'Naga. How long, she wondered, would it have taken if it had been necessary for her to travel this distance alone?

The sky was brightening and below them she could see nothing but endless blue water. Dollops of white like drops of whipped cream covered it. She could see no land. How long could Api'Naga continue like this without rest? They had never flown so far or so long.

She leaned forward and sent the question. — How long?

The answer was instant like a whoosh of air through her head. **As long as I must.**

She smiled and sat back. She should have known. She had always been the one that stopped them. Too tired, too cold, too hungry, too...too much of the human in her. The sunrays broke above the horizon washing the waves in the distance with gold.

Another whoosh. **If you like, there is land there beyond the line of your sight. It may even be the land you seek.**

She rubbed her hand on the rough back. Yes. She leaned forward, put her head on her arms. She might as well rest. If it was the place then there was no knowing what awaited and she would need all the strength she could muster. Api'Naga could go long distances but would need rest too and so it would be up to her to do the initial reconnoiter. She had nothing — no maps, no background. Only a name. Why did her first assignment have to be this one?

"You will go to the other side of tomorrow and find..."

Kour'el woke up feeling sick and afraid. Someone was in the room. She had heard something, some almost imperceptible stirring. A rustling? Somewhere. Where?

It was dark, not night yet but she had obviously slept a long time as the room was in deep shadow.

There it was again. She had to strain to hear it. A rustling sound. A familiar rustling sound.

But so faint, why was it so faint? And why was it so familiar? She listened, staring into the darkness. Perhaps next time she could make out where in the room it had come from. Somewhere above her. But then everything was above her lying flat here on the pallet. She didn't dare move in case she frightened it.

A mouse perhaps? No, that would not have aroused such a strong feeling in her. She was used to this sound but bigger, stronger. She remembered the moan she had heard earlier and wondered if they were connected. Somehow she was sure that they were. One thing was certain. She was no longer alone.

It seemed forever that she sat there waiting for the sound to be repeated. The blackness was intense now. She could see nothing in the room. No shapes. And she gave up and closed her eyes. Perhaps if she slept again she would dream another piece of the past. Another piece of the puzzle.

She awakened to bright daylight. The sun was almost to the mark on the wall. She felt dull and lethargic. And very disappointed. There had been no dream, at least nothing she could remember.

It took all her strength to prop herself up on her elbow and look around the room. Nothing had changed. Whatever had made the rustling sound must be so very small it could hide amidst the cracks in the stone. It was completely hidden — or gone.

In a few moments she would know if the old woman would come again. There were only a few sips of water left in the ewer. She would save them until later. And after that? She did not want to think about after that.

And then the door opened and the old woman entered. She was carrying a besom and nothing else. She said nothing as always, did not look at Kour'el but proceeded to sweep up the broken pitcher swiftly, her movements abrupt. She is angry, Kour'el thought and realized that it was the first time she was aware of any emotion from the woman. It alarmed her. Would she be punished for breaking the pitcher? Another day without food — without water? The thought was unbearable but Kour'el held her tongue. She knew instinctively an apology would not help and might make matters worse.

The rattle of the twig broom against the stone floor, the clatter of the pieces of broken pitcher were the loudest things she'd heard since she'd been here and seemed overwhelming. Even the crash of the pitcher breaking had not seemed to dominate the place like this did. The woman swept the pieces out through the door and closed it behind her. Kour'el's heart sank. And then from somewhere on the wall above her she heard the faint moan again. Before she could turn to look the door opened again and the old woman reappeared this time carrying a pitcher and the ewer which she placed on the stand, dropped a stiff curtsy and left.

Food! Water! Kour'el almost wept with joy. Instantly she felt ashamed — she was supposed to be one of the brave ones. The moment she thought that, she was surprised. Her identity in the dreams was becoming more real. Part of her. She rose stiffly and made her way slowly across the room. It did not seem so difficult now. There was food waiting and she would be strong again soon. The old woman had left no bread today. Perhaps the bread and soup were meant to do her for two days. If she had not broken the pitcher and lost so much it might have been enough. Perhaps the staying away was not punishment for having broken it after all? But no, the old woman had been angry she was sure of that. Angry about something.

But the curtsy had been the same as always. It flashed through her mind that whatever angered the old woman, the anger might not be directed at her and she felt some relief at that.

She drank most of the broth and picked up a piece of the meat. She wanted to bolt it down but knew that her former habit of rationing had been wise. She would be careful and just in case, she fished out over half of the remaining meat and set it on the wooden stand.

And now because she had eaten she felt strong again. Not only that but her mind had cleared and she remembered. The sounds from yesterday and the moan this morning. Where had they come from? Somewhere above her, but her attention had been focused on the old woman and the worry of what she would do another day without food. Perhaps if she lay down again and pretended to sleep she might hear something again. She lay very still.

Yes! There it was — the rustling sound. But it was hard to pinpoint where it came from, lying on her side like this.

Very close. She opened her eyes. Had the noise just been her eyelash rubbing against the sturdy canvas of the pallet? She rolled painfully onto her back and closed her eyes again. Listening with all her might.

Again. From somewhere above her. So soft. Something very tiny. A moth? Even a moth would be something to look at, something to pass the hours. She did not want to sleep again until night. But the sound didn't come again. And without meaning to she slept.

For the time being the girls were herded into the large room where the elders of the village met from time to time. Maighdlin and Mala stood close together as far from the door as they could get. Mala had ceased crying.

Maighdlin wanted to ask her where she'd thought she could hide. Even now the soldiers, except for those guarding the door, had begun to search from house to house. She looked around to see who might be missing. Which girl might have understood the meaning of the proclamation soon enough to escape or not to have been there at all? Who lived farthest away? She could tell that other girls were doing the same. In fact she could hear a murmur of talk from some of them as they speculated aloud. She was alarmed. They shouldn't do that. The two soldiers guarding just inside the door might have their backs to them but they could hear. It was exactly the sort of thing they would be trying to do.

She had to distract them, drown out the talk.

"Quick Mala! Sing!"

Mala looked at her in alarm. "Are you mad?" She hissed. "You know I have a voice that makes the bush parrot sound like a fairy wren!" She laughed a little through her tears. "You are a strange one, Maighdlin. *You* want singing? *You* sing!"

Maighdlin heart sank. It would have to be her. Her

voice was sweet and true, but not strong. Perhaps if some of the others joined in it would be enough to drown out the talk. It should be something rousing — but her mind was blank. The vessel song was out of the question. Although it was not forbidden, she had heard that Queen Mariah had built great armed fortresses at all the harbors in the land so that no ship could dock. That song might only make the captain angry. She could think of nothing but a lament. And maybe that was appropriate too, at least for Brede's Marika, still sobbing softly. That gave her an idea. She took a deep breath.

"They have taken my love and my sorrow is deep..."
The talk ceased and the room was instantly quiet. Maighdlin had always been shy about her voice and had held back when others sang. But she often sang to herself when spinning or rocking young Bron. Now her lilting voice soared, lifted, filling the vaulted room, so different from the cottage or the blanket-partitioned corner where she and her brother slept. She surprised herself. She surprised the others in the room. And the soldiers at the door turned to look, half in curiosity at who it was and half in amazement.

Please somebody, she thought, sing with me. I can't keep this up. To her surprise the voice that joined her, though catching on the words so that they fell like tears, was Marika's.

"For my arms are so empty, and it's lonely to weep..."
One or two other voices had begun to sing. Softly like an accompaniment. And another girl whom Maighdlin recognized as the musician's daughter suddenly began a descant that swept over and through the melody Maighdlin sang. And Mala, yes, even Mala sang. Maighdlin smiled at her

gratefully. Her voice was not like a bush parrot at all but deep with a rumbling hoarseness that reminded Maighdlin of far distant thunder and somehow blended in with the other voices.

And then something happened that had not even occurred to Maighdlin. Like thunder coming closer, men's and women's voices from outside joined in, swelling the song. She had not realized the people were still outside; parents, brothers and friends still standing in the square. Inside they had felt cut off, torn away from their loved ones and it must have been that way too for their families, for her mother standing holding Bron. Now because of the song they were somehow together, bound by their voices, by the lament. Their song of sorrow.

She could hear the captain shouting but the singing just seemed to get louder. The song was finished but someone started it again. It would go on for a long time. It went on until the soldiers moved the girls out again and began herding them down the road out of the village towards the next village on the winding road to the palace so many miles away. But the people followed still singing.

Maighdlin caught a glimpse of her mother and Bron and knew that her mother could not follow far. She hoped GranDa would not be told until tomorrow or at least until the soldiers were gone. She did not want him coming trying to rescue her. She felt a shiver of fear when she remembered the beautiful thing that Bron had found. What if the searching soldiers...? No, she calmed herself, GranDa would have hidden it well as soon as she left. And the soldiers were searching for girls, nothing else. It would be safe. And GranDa too.

When the last straggling villagers who followed had turned back the singing stopped. The girls needed all their breath to keep up the pace the soldiers demanded of them. Maighdlin recognized the young soldier walking beside her — it was the one who had let her be in the village, the one who'd quietly walked without pushing or touching her. The captain had spaced the soldiers to march alongside each row of girls, and this one had moved up so that he walked beside the three or four girls in Maighdlin's row.

It seemed to Maighdlin that there were a ridiculously large allotment of soldiers to guard a few unarmed girls but she supposed that the show of force was necessary to prevent their families and loved ones from trying to free them. Other girls and soldiers joined them at the next village and they were able to snatch a bit of a rest as they waited. Not enough. The soldiers were efficient and they moved off soon.

She tried not to think about what would happen. Would she ever see GranDa and Bron and her mother again? She knew she had to put such thoughts from her mind and concentrate on her walking. They were in strange country now. She had never in her fourteen years been beyond the next village. The land was becoming more hilly, the road steeper, though now it was paved with cobblestone. That too made the walking harder.

><+>-O-<+><

Petaurus did not find out until the next day. The soldiers had not come as far as his cottage for the search had been discontinued. When the singing began the captain feared what might happen and made haste to take those girls he had away. It would be enough.

The old man had risen before daybreak, gathered some bread and cheese into a large kerchief, tied it in a knapsack and set out down the hill to his daughter's hut in the village. He realized he had not been down there for many, many years — not since Maighdlin was old enough to fetch him the simple food her mother sent. Not far down the path he met his daughter, her face streaked with tears. His heart stopped.

"The girl?" He said as soon as he was close enough.
But the shock of seeing him so far from his hut, leaning heavily on his gnarled walking stick, rendered the woman speechless. He spoke again, urgently. "Maighdlin? What has become of her?"

"Father, you know? How could you know?" Her voice was breathless, and she shifted the boy she was carrying.

It took some moments before the story was clear. Before he became aware of the horror of what had happened.

"The king cannot possibly know," he muttered. "He would never allow such a thing."

When King Vassill had been well there was never a need to conscript servants for the palace. It had been an honor to work there and always young men and maidens from the villages would vie with each other to be chosen. And the young people would return with money enough to marry and begin families. In the years since the king's accident, however, those who went into service were never seen or heard from again. At first people thought it was because they preferred to stay and live in the city surrounding the palace and there had been many a parent much hurt by this. But in later years rumors began that the servants were no more than slaves, ill-treated, starved and never given their freedom even if they lived. So no one went willingly to apply.

"But why were you coming down to the village if you did not know?"

Petaurus shook his head sadly. He was not going to the village. He was going beyond, far beyond. Somehow he must get to the palace. He must get to his old friend, the king. He had wondered how he would explain this trip for no one must know his real purpose. And no one must know of the beautiful fragment he had carefully tucked into the hem of the sleeve of his old shirt.

He tried to sound as casual as he could. "I thought it was time I ventured farther than just from bench to bed, lest my old bones seize up entirely. And the day is fine."

They had begun walking. Slowly, for young Bron now wandered on his own and while he could easily have out-walked his grandfather, his route was erratic, now on the path, now off to chase a butterfly or squat to poke at a bug. "What are the people doing?" He questioned partly because he wanted to know and partly to distract his daughter from his unusual behavior. There had been fine days in the past, and the danger of old bones seizing up, yet these had not inspired him to walk even so far as the village.

"Mourning, mostly. Some from true sorrow and some, like the miller, from not having a strong worker at his beck and call."

The old man sighed. "There is nothing they can do. Nothing."

The woman laughed bitterly. "There is one who is determined to follow...all anyone can do is try to persuade him to wait until his wounds heal. Young Brede is set to go to the city and lurk about the palace until he can find and steal his Marika back." She sighed. "It is hoped that some of the older wise men can talk some sense into him and make him see that he must give up such foolishness and stay." Her face brightened. "Perhaps he would listen to you...since you're coming to the village anyway."

"Perhaps," was all he replied, saving his breath for the walk.

He would talk to Brede. But he would not try to persuade him to stay — only to take a companion. Traveling with a strong young man would be useful. They could use the excuse of taking things to the city market to sell for the villagers. That had not been done since the beginning of the time of woe either. He felt himself walking more quickly and he hoped it was his resolve giving him strength and not just the downhill slope of the path. Even the disaster of Maighdlin's capture might work for him. It would not hurt to have a smart granddaughter living in the palace. And if Brede could smuggle one girl out, perhaps another could be freed as well.

Chapter Eleven

———

Kour'el's first thought was that she must be losing her mind. She knew she had placed those pieces of meat on the stand *beside* the pitcher before she lay down. She had not slept long — the sunlight was not far from the mark on the wall. And yet there was nothing there. Not a scrap.

How could that be? People did go mad from being locked up alone, she'd heard. But she could not let herself believe that. She must believe her eyes. The meat had been there and now it was not. Something had taken it. Something had taken those bits on the floor when the pitcher broke. They had not evaporated. Twice, it had happened — it was not her imagination. She might have written off the sounds alone but not both things. There was something here. She circled the room checking everywhere for a hole — a crack in the mortar of the stones that might have been big enough for a mouse — but there was nothing. It could have been a bird. One could fly in the window. That must be it. Whatever it was, it could not take the meat from the pitcher, only from the floor or the stand.

She fished the last pieces of meat out of the pitcher, ate some of the vegetables and most of the meat and placed the last two morsels on the stand. Then very quietly she went back to the pallet and lay down facing the stand. She lowered her eyelids to look as if she were asleep and watched. She did not have to wait long. Something glided from the window and landed without a sound beside the food. It was very small. Not much bigger than her finger. Not a moth though the tiny wings had that iridescence — a strangely beautiful, very tiny bat, perhaps?

She watched stone-still, fascinated. The pieces of meat were almost half the size of the creature and yet it began to devour them. And then she almost gasped with amazement for with every bite the creature expanded visibly, its growth in exact proportion to what it was eating. Now she could see the tiny head and eyes more clearly. It was not a bat. The head was larger, differently shaped, and the wings were not batlike. Soon the meat was gone. And then the tiny creature glided to the floor and began to climb with wings and feet slowly and painstakingly up the stone wall opposite her. It took some time and she watched not daring to breathe. At last it reached the top and then turned and began a slanting downwards glide toward her.

Kour'el couldn't help it. She gasped and moved involuntarily, though as she did so she realized that the target of the glide was much higher than her pallet. It was obviously aiming for the stones of the windowledge. She heard the landing and waited, hoping she hadn't alarmed the tiny — what should she call it? It was not feathered like a bird.

She stood up and crossed the room to the stand. One little drink of water wouldn't hurt though she usually waited until later in the day. She turned casually as she drank, peering over the edge of the ewer. She did not want to startle it. If it flew through the window she might not see it again.

It was still there. Perched on the windowledge on this side of the bars. She would love to drag the stand over to the window and climb up again — she was sure she was strong enough now — amazing how quickly the meat had restored her strength — but she wouldn't. She might frighten it. Better to pretend that she wasn't interested. Tame it with food.

She crossed again to the pallet and lay down. She felt full of life and excitement, just as she had when she and Api'Naga had set out on this trip. Knowing she had a companion. She shivered with anticipation. The days would not be so long and dreary now. Even a companion so little was something to watch. She would be patient and tame it. She would have a friend. A friend to talk to while she waited.

She sat up suddenly. It was the first time she had acknowledged that. She was waiting. Waiting for what? At first it had been to get well, to get her strength back but now she realized she was waiting for something else. That was why she hadn't despaired in spite of the hopelessness of her imprisonment.

She closed her eyes, smiling to herself as she fell asleep.

Flames...flames all around her. The sound again not from outside, another voice, but a scream exploding in her head. A scream more terrible than anything she had ever known. And the pain in her back, tearing her, and the knowledge as she lost consciousness that Api'Naga was dead.

She woke up sobbing. She knew now why she'd blocked out everything. Not the pain or the injuries or even fear of whoever had brought her here. It was the despair of knowing. She had lost Api'Naga. The one who'd saved her from her mistakes, comforted and guided her. Gone.

She had gone to sleep hopeful and happy. Awakening, she had to acknowledge the terrible truth, the truth she hadn't dared face before.

She looked in the pitcher and ate the last few pieces of stringy vegetables. There were two morsels of meat she'd missed. She could see the little creature still perched on the window ledge. She took one piece in her hand, crossed the room and placed it on the opposite end of the sill. She couldn't see when she stood like this on tiptoe so she left it and went back to the stand. Good. The creature had moved over and almost before she turned was eating. She waited until it settled again, then slowly began to carry the stand across the room. She didn't want to drag it and risk the noise so it took awhile. She positioned the stand at the side of the window opposite to where she'd last seen the — she would have to name it soon, she could not just keep calling it "creature".

Slowly, as quietly as she could, she climbed onto the stand.

She hoped that the appearance of her head wouldn't startle it too much. The last thing she wanted was to disturb it or frighten it so that it flew away, out the window. What if it could not get back? It had taken so long to go up the little wall of this room. To climb the outside wall would take much too long.

She moved very slowly and was pleased to see that she had indeed chosen the right side of the window. The little creature — though now it was more than twice as big as it had been when she first saw it — was huddled in the shadow, tucked behind one of the bars so that part of its head was hidden. She tried not to look directly at it. She did not want to seem threatening. She should talk to it, she supposed, but the Watcher might also be able to hear and she did not want to risk anyone recognizing the importance to her of this new companion. Already she could feel desolation at the mere thought of losing it.

She placed the last piece of meat on the stone ledge halfway between them. And waited. It began to move the moment her hand was withdrawn — she wondered if it would have come anyway, even to have taken the food from her hand.

Now she could see it clearly, the shape of its legs, its tail, the delicate iridescence of the wings. She gasped. It was so small — and yet somehow familiar.

It finished eating, and now slightly larger began to back up towards the corner.

Woosh. Softly so that she could hardly hear. Thank you.

It was not a voice outside. She was not hearing with her ears. The voice was inside her head.

The shock of recognition was so great she almost spoke the name aloud. Api'Naga! She should have recognized it earlier but Api'Naga was so huge she was more familiar with parts of him — the broad back, the sweeping wings, the noble head.

She sent the words without thinking. — You are like a very little Api'Naga.

She felt tears coming at the thought of her loss. It would be painful having this tiny reminder around.

Yes, came the answer in her head.

She almost laughed out loud. The Watcher might see what she saw, or perhaps nothing more than a large mantis-like insect. But the Watcher would hear nothing. Even she had to listen with great concentration, the voice was so small. So unlike Api'Naga, who'd always had to tone it down so as not to fill her head to bursting with his rumbling voice. Like the sound, the last terrible cry when he had died. A cry that was silent to everyone but her.

— Oh I am so happy you are here! she sent. You are like... She stopped. She did not even want to mention anything that would bring back the sorrow.

And then gently, very gently came the response. **I am Api'Naga.**

She shook her head. The little thing could read her thoughts and she'd been thinking Api'Naga's name. No. This was not possible and it shocked her — it was almost blasphemous to think such a thing. — Don't...

But her sending was interrupted. **I am Api'Naga...Kour'el.** She could tell it was using all its energy to send the message strongly. **I have come back to you.**

CHAPTER TWELVE

———·+·———

Brede's wounds were not serious. The arm that had been slashed was bound with herbs by Marika's mother, the healing woman of the village. When Petaurus finally arrived it was obvious that even she was attempting to dissuade him.

"No one wants her back more than I do, Brede," she said, as she rubbed salve on the other cuts. "But you must see that it is foolish to waste your life." She turned and, seeing Petaurus, tried to hide her amazement. "You talk to him, Old One...I can't..." her voice choked and she quickly left the room.

Petaurus nodded. Her eyes, like his daughter's, were red with weeping. The whole village had an air of shock and sorrow as if there had been a massacre of its young. And indeed to them there might as well have been.

Brede looked at the old man with the air of one who is willing to listen but determined not to be swayed. He had already dealt with friends and family.

Petaurus pointed to the young man's swollen jaw for there were not only sword wounds but a darkened eye and other marks on his face. "Did they beat you too?" was all he said.

The young man showed his surprise and then smiled ruefully. "Not the soldiers...my *friends* did this." He fingered a split lip. "A little enthusiastic in their attempts to keep me from attacking the soldiers again".

"Your friends were right to stop you. You are of no use to the maiden if you are dead."

The older man paused, letting the meaning sink in. He could tell the youth was puzzled — this was not the approach he expected. But Brede was wary, still waiting for the attempt to dissuade him. Petaurus lowered himself wearily onto a stool, wondering briefly if he would be able to rise again.

The young man shifted uneasily, waiting. Finally he burst out, "I am going to go. No one can stop me!"

It was some time before Petaurus spoke again. "I was very familiar with the palace in the days when the king was still well." He stopped again, rubbing his beard thoughtfully. He could tell the young man was impatient and somewhat thrown by this strange new direction of talk but he said nothing, the old man's calm voice and manner relaxing him a little.

"How do you plan to travel?" Petaurus asked at last.

Brede looked shocked and it was obvious he had given no more thought to this than just impetuously setting out on the road.

Petaurus spoke again, weighing his words. "It would probably be best if you took a cart of goods to the city for the market. Perhaps your father would let you take his." He paused once more watching the young man absorb this.

Brede looked at him suspiciously, "You are not going to try to talk me out of going?"

Petaurus chose not to answer directly. "An old man and a young one with a cart full of produce..." he went on as if talking to himself, "...that would not attract too much attention...and unless things have changed a great deal there would still be a great many people in the market-place. We would not be noticed in the crowd." He did not even look at Brede but appeared to be intent on rubbing a callus on his finger.

Slowly the bruised face broadened into a grin. "You're not here to talk me out of going at all!" He burst out laughing. "You want to come along!"

Petaurus wondered about young Brede. He didn't know the young people of the village these days and he wasn't sure what kind of young man he was dealing with. Brave and a little foolhardy, to judge from recent behavior. He would find out what sort of youth Brede was by his response now. And if impetuosity was the predominant characteristic it would be just as well not to go with him. He realized the young man was looking at him seriously now.

"Young Maighdlin used to talk of her wise brave GranDa," he said, "and I'll admit we laughed and teased her a bit. But she was right — *you* are right. It would not do to set out alone with no obvious purpose, for people would soon assume the worst." He stopped, sizing up the old man. "The palace may have changed since your day," he said gently.

Petaurus nodded, relief swelling inside. The young man was no fool. He could see wisdom and think things through. And the bravery he had shown in attempting to save his bride-to-be could be channeled. There might be hope for both their ventures. He gestured toward the injured arm. "How long did the healer say it would be before it's safe for you to be about?"

"Hard to say... her advice was intended to keep me here..." the young man smiled again. "It will take a day or two to gather produce and ready the cart...once we persuade my father to let us take it."

Petaurus nodded. "It may not be easy to gather anything. Our people quit going to the city many years ago when neither goods nor vendors returned."

"But they'll know our real purpose and while they might not have supported me, perhaps for you..." Brede smiled at him. "You are sure this will not be too much? I thought...I thought you were too crippled even to come down to the village."

"Sometimes you just have to try...to see what you can do. It's easy enough to sit in the sun at the door of a hut and wait for a granddaughter to break up your day for you." He rose stiffly, a little amazed that he was able to stand up at all and leaning on his cane walked to the door. "You will rest and do everything Marika's mother asks of you today. And I will pay a little visit to your father...your grandfather and I hunted together many times, you know."

Brede settled back on his cushions. "Tell that good woman to come back with her sleeping potion," he called, "I'll take it now." And softly, Petaurus heard, "Go well, Grandfather."

CHAPTER THIRTEEN

No! It couldn't be true! The Great One was dead. She had accepted that death. She knew it was true beyond any doubt. She knew the great ones would sometimes grow a new leg or tail if one was accidently severed but this was different. Yet all the time her mind argued against it, her instinct told her it was true. It made no sense, but here he was. It must be Api'Naga, for this little creature had known her name. She may have thought his name but she would never have thought her own. He *had* known.

There were so many questions she wanted to ask but she had sensed a weakness, a terrible weariness, and he had crept slowly back — dragged himself back to the place behind the bar, in the shadow, almost out of sight.

She stood staring out the window. The lake below shone golden now. It must be sunset for the barren brown hills beyond were tinged in pinks and violets reflected in the clouds too. It was beautiful. Kour'el felt happier than she had in a long time. Happier perhaps than in her whole life. A wide-winged seabird drifted lazily in the sky, lifting effortlessly, soaring free. She envied it that flight and not just the freedom of it. The flight itself seemed to evoke a longing deeper than pain.

— Sleep well, she sent, but the little Api'Naga was obviously already sleeping soundly.

She climbed down and moved the stand back across the

room as quietly as she could. Her back bothered her. Aching. She leaned it against the cool stones of the wall. That seemed to help. She looked back across the room. From here she could hardly see anything in that darkened corner. If she had not known she would have thought it was just a shadow. The old woman would not notice. The old woman *must* not notice.

At last, as the shadows increased, she crossed to her pallet again. Her back still bothered her, part of the injury from that terrible day. Or had it been night? Her nightmarish memories were filled only with sound and pain. What had led up to it? She had few enough pieces to the puzzle even now. But when Api'Naga was stronger they could talk. Even the pain in her back could not keep her from a feeling of blissful contentment. And she had tomorrow to look forward to. For the first time she would sleep looking forward to waking. Her mind was full of resolve. She could manage with only half the meat if the old woman brought bread too. If the old woman *came* tomorrow. She pushed that thought away. She would not waste energy worrying. Sleep was what was needed now.

She was tired very, very tired. They had arrived and while Api'Naga slept hidden she had climbed to a high place to find what the land was like.

The island was beautiful. Rocky cliffs in places, gentle beaches that sparkled white in the sun, coves and inlets and spits of land covered with flowering trees. The perfume that had drifted up to them as they flew low to land had been almost overpowering. Hypnotic. It left her drowsy even though she had slept as they flew. It left the Great One lying senseless almost as soon as they landed. There were villages to be seen on the rolling hilly inland plains and now and then a stone fortress. She saw nothing of the great Amethyst Palace she'd been told to look for. They had avoided all signs of life and found a quiet spot to stop where the tall trees with bark like strings would hide them for awhile.

She realized they would have to travel at night if they were to avoid being seen. Meanwhile she would go on foot and to avoid attracting attention she wrapped a dark cloak around herself. It was light but it covered her. Clothing, even the people themselves, might be different. And she did not want to appear too strange should she meet someone. She kept to the forest, pushing through the thick flowering bushes. The heavy scent made her drowsy but she dared not stop, let alone sit down. At last she came to a steep cliff above a lake. If she went up there she could see everywhere, she thought. Almost as good as flying. But the way was steep, and the path disappeared from time to time leaving nothing but the sheer cliff face.

At the top, the path ended against a stone wall that circled the top of the cliff as far as she could see. She slumped down, too exhausted to begin the long climb down. She would rest and then move on when she regained her strength. She continued to watch down the path. It would not do to cease vigilance — someone might have followed her. She made herself comfortable, hidden by some thick bushes, her back to the stone wall, her cloak wrapped around her against the chill wind.

She felt secure — sitting still, her back pressed against

the sun-warmed stones, the bushes sheltering her. It would be all right to rest here a little longer. If only she could resist the temptation to sleep.

And then, without warning, the wall behind her moved, pushing her and she felt herself falling.

CHAPTER FOURTEEN

It took three days for Petaurus to make things ready. Brede's father resisted only briefly. He was old enough to remember and respect the man Petaurus had been. As for the village, at first people were reluctant to send anything to market so far away — it had been years since anyone had seen the profit of going. But either their sorrow for a lost daughter or the wish for someone brave enough to do something — anything — made each of them feel they must contribute something. The miller amazed everyone with five sacks of grain, the butcher with a crate of chickens.

Petaurus amazed himself. The more he moved from place to place, hut to hut, the easier it seemed. His hobble changed to a walk, slow to be sure, but firm and steady. Some of it he knew was the herbal ointment supplied by Marika's mother that he rubbed on his legs each night. Some was the exercise he was taking after so many years of sitting hour after hour. But he truly believed most of the improvement was because, for the first time since the despair over the king's accident, he had a purpose, a goal — and perhaps, though he hardly dared believe it, some hope.

For his part Brede relaxed as much as possible and allowed himself to be ministered to by Marika's mother with all the healing power she possessed. Even she was amazed by his quick recovery, though she told him it was in part simply the ability of a strong young body to heal itself once allowed to rest.

When their cart reached the next village, word had spread and so many wanted to send produce that Petaurus had to refuse lest the donkeys that pulled them become overburdened. He comforted people by saying that they would take their offerings on the next trip. For he had decided that if they were unsuccessful in their quest after a week or so in the city they would return and try again rather than stay too long and attract suspicion.

⊱┈⟡┈○┈⟡┈⊰

Maighdlin and the other girls travelled more and more slowly as they neared the city. The soldiers were more lenient as they realized that the villagers showed more resentment than resistance and the captain relaxed understanding this was not a battle campaign and that it was not useful to march the girls too far or too fast each day. Fainting girls had to be gathered up and carried. Provisions were not a problem either, since the villages were forced to supply food. This meant the villages closest the city suffered the most as they not only lost their daughters but had to feed the soldiers and the daughters of all the other villages, using up much of the food they needed to get them through the winter. People remembered when the king's men would have paid them for the food they took, and mourned the weakness that took their king from them.

The last night out from the city they camped on the hillside above the poorest village of all. Threats had extorted little, so the meal the girls shared as they huddled about the fire was simply roasted potatoes. Still, Maighdlin thought, an exhausted Mala lying beside her, that was the least of their worries. Her feet were aching and blistered from walking in her worn old sandals. Many of the girls were suffering from sunstroke and she felt nauseous too. She'd given her headscarf to Mala whose light coloring made her much more prone to burn. She wondered if she would have made it through the day at all if the young soldier had not moved her to the edge of the ranks of girls and thus given her the chance to walk in the shade of the trees that lined the roadway. She had learned his name now from hearing it called out by one of his fellows when they had stopped for the night. Talun.

He must come from a village far from her own. Each village was required to use the initials of its own name in naming its children. In her own — Blue Mountain — the boys were named with B, the girls with M. It had not always been so. In GranDa's day any name could be chosen. But Queen Mariah wished to have people easily traced. Talun must have come from somewhere on the other edge of the kingdom, there were no villages with T's nearby. She wondered how long it was since he'd been taken from his home. Surely no one volunteered any more.

Mala moaned softly in her sleep and Maighdlin huddled closer to her. They had no blankets and since the day they'd been taken had been warm, few of them had come away with shawls. Marika was one of the few, and she came and lay beside the two younger girls, spreading her shawl over the three of them. Maighdlin smiled gratefully and closed her eyes. For some reason the older girl had befriended her though they'd not known each other well at home, living at opposite ends of the village and having the difference in age. Perhaps it was the song that had done it, Maighdlin thought sleepily. Whatever the reason she was grateful.

The city was a complete surprise to her. From a distance the walls could be seen, dark and imposing. No trees or bushes lined the cobbled roadway so that the city rose out of barrenness. No grass or flowers grew on the hillside where it stood. The road had widened and they shared it now with carts carrying produce to market. It seemed to Maighdlin to be unnaturally quiet. No one shouted or talked. The men walked beside their carts sullenly and did not greet each other. It was as if the people did not exist, only the creaking carts, the clattering hooves. The girls were too tired to speak even if the captain had not that very morning forbidden them to do so. Maighdlin looked over at Mala whose milky white skin seemed even paler than usual. She moved closer to her friend and took her arm trying to give her some support.

GranDa had described the city to her so often she felt she would walk into a familiar place. But as they entered the gates she was horrified. She had expected noise and people milling about, for the square inside the gate was the marketplace. She'd looked forward to seeing the stalls selling everything from food to fine silks and spices from far away. When GranDa had talked of it she could almost smell the cinnamon and cloves and rich perfumes — boronia and jasmine mingling in the warm summer air.

Instead she was assaulted by a horrible rotting smell that made her gasp and cover her nose. There was no sound of laughter or shouts from the vendors, only an ominous rumble of grumbling talk. Quarreling everywhere. Voices that seemed too tired to fight and too angry to agree.

76

As they moved further in she could see the source of the awful odor. Beggars, dead and dying, ringed the market area. Above them, on the parapets, the bodies of gibbeted men, some newly dead, some hanging in rags, like scarecrows, were being pecked by the carrion birds. She felt the gorge rising in her throat. Others did throw up. It was such a brutal change from the fresh summer air they had been breathing.

She was supporting Mala completely now, grateful at least that her friend seemed oblivious to the horror around them. They were crowded together, squeezing through the stalls to the street beyond and it was difficult to see. The stones were slippery underfoot and Maighdlin did not want to know what it was that made them so. She stumbled and would have fallen but a strong arm was around her, steadying her so that the weight of Mala would not pull her down. She knew without looking that it was Talun, murmured, "Thank you" keeping her eyes straight ahead not wanting to call attention to his kindness. He continued to hold her until they had moved into the clearer street beyond.

Now, as they climbed and turned a corner she could see the Amethyst Palace of the king and queen. GranDa had described it often. It was not, of course, made of amethyst but enough of the crystals had been embedded in the stones around the entryway to dazzle in the sunlight and lend the palace their name. She could see *that* at least had not changed.

Suddenly the captain shouted a command, and they were herded into a side street — more like an alley — where the stone buildings seemed to meet overhead and block out the sun. Maighdlin could see a procession coming from the palace gates, hear the fanfare of trumpets. Quietly as if speaking to himself Talun explained. "The queen is making her weekly progress through the city...part of the city...."

"Kneel!" ordered the captain.

Maighdlin looked for a clean spot to kneel and realized that the stones here had been freshly swept; indeed tubs of sweet-smelling flowers were everywhere. But even the perfume of nearby roses failed to erase the stench that still lingered in Maighdlin's nostrils. The "part of the city" the queen saw was obviously not the one they had just walked through.

She inched over so that she could see between the kneeling girls ahead of her. Queen Mariah was, as GranDa said, the most beautiful woman in the world. She looked no older than her daughters, walking behind her. Her striking brown eyes and dark hair, perfectly coifed beneath the sparkling tiara she wore, made the princesses, for all their lovely long curling hair, pale in comparison. The queen neither smiled nor waved her daintily gloved hands, but her eyes seemed to sweep the crowd. And there was something in the queen's eyes, for all their beauty, that sent a shudder through Maighdlin and caused her to look down until the procession had gone by.

"Move on!" came the order and she struggled to rise.

Mala had slumped into a faint and Maighdlin hoped it was merely from exhaustion as she tried to rouse her friend. Again, quietly, without drawing attention to it, Talun was there lifting Mala to her feet. Maighdlin was grateful when Marika came and with one of them on either side they were able to propel her along. The captain seemed desperate to complete the last short distance to the palace before the procession returned.

Once inside they were herded into a small courtyard, with barely floor space to crouch down, and here it appeared they must wait, with the sun beating down, until someone from the palace decided where to put them. Again Marika's shawl served well as they took turns holding it up as a sunshade over themselves and the now unconscious Mala. Luckily there was a small fountain and they were able to drink. Maighdlin wet her handkerchief to wipe Mala's feverish forehead. Two soldiers were assigned at either doorway. One was Talun.

So they waited until nightfall.

CHAPTER FIFTEEN

A voice woke her, crying out. Her own voice. Kour'el lay on the pallet trembling. Once again she could not go beyond the dream.

There was a tiny plop on the pallet beside her head. And she smelled very faintly the sharp piney smell she had always associated with her friend. She was instantly awake and very frightened.

Are you all right? The words came faintly into her head.

Api'Naga's concern brought tears to her eyes but he must not risk being seen. Last night she was sure he could not have been observed by whoever watched her. It had been twilight and she thought that, because of his size, he would have been nearly invisible in the dim light. But now, it was bright daylight — and, she noticed with shock, he was over twice as big as he'd been then. Nearly the size of one of the birds she remembered from home — a lark perhaps?

She propped herself on her elbows trying to hide him, wondering once again where the Watcher's peephole could be and what angle she should try to shade him from.

— Don't show yourself. She sent the words quickly. I am watched. I don't know how, but things that happen here while I'm alone are known. She waited as he crept beneath her. — I'm sorry I alarmed you. It was a dream. I have forgotten nearly everything but sometimes I dream a piece of it.

She looked up and saw with shock that the sun had reached the mark she'd made on the wall. — Don't move, she sent and at that moment the door opened and the old woman entered. She carried, as Kour'el had hoped, the small loaf of bread as well as the pitcher of soup and the ewer of water but Kour'el tried to compose her face in the usual way, neither expressing hope nor fear. She remained still, watching the woman as she crossed the room and placed the things on the stand. Everything must be as usual, the old woman must not suspect.

She did not seem to for she gave Kour'el the usual curtsy. As always Kour'el could see nothing of her face, only the gnarled hands that carried the empty pitcher and ewer. Trying to think of something other than her hidden friend, Kour'el noticed how small the twisted hands were. Once, she thought with a shock, they must have been smooth and dainty, beautiful even. She looked curiously at the old woman. There was grace in the curtsy despite the stiffness of it. Why had she not observed that before?

She stayed as she was, propped on her elbows, her head twisted to watch the door close behind the old woman. Then, rather awkwardly, she brought her hands together, cupping Api'Naga inside and sat up. She raised her hands to the moon-shape she had designed on the wall and rose smoothly to walk toward it, hands above her prayerfully. She stood there awhile posing for the Watcher.

— I will put you back on the windowledge and you must stay there until twilight. I'll bring you food, she thought to him as she turned and, hands still upraised, went to the window. She had never made obeisance to the sun before, only her moon drawing, but decided she would add this to the ritual — she would need a way to carry food unseen to the window.

Thank you... came the faint response, I am strangely hungry.

Kour'el smiled. That was good. A tiny Api'Naga, while a good companion, would not be of much help. Larger and stronger he could fly out and tell her where she was imprisoned, what was nearby, even how the door was secured.

She returned to the food on the stand and drank the broth, carefully separating the meat as she always did. There was much to think about. Yesterday her only thought had been rationing the food for survival — now she could dream of escape. Questions crowded in on her. For the first time she wondered why she was being held here, kept alive. For what purpose? There were problems too, she realized as she returned to the window, two pieces of meat between her clasped hands. Now that Api'Naga was larger he would be noticeable — when would he be strong enough to fly again? And could he fly again? Did not the Great Ones swallow the rocks from their home mountains to make the heat and smoke to lift them so that their wings could propel them about?

She had forgotten that her thinking could be heard. You have observed more of my kind than I realized, young one. Even in the weakness of the voice she could recognize some of the old teasing amusement at her. It is true, we need the gray rocks that people call limestone to create the chemistry to make fire and fly, but I have observed several of these embedded in your wall. If you could scratch away some bits... She sensed a sigh. Though I fear you will tear your fingernails and it will be in vain.

Kour'el thought of the sharp shards of pitcher that she had hidden in her pallet. — I can do it easily! When do you want me to begin? She was eager to be of help, eager for the long period of doing nothing to be over.

The voice in her head was weak indeed. All the effort was obviously tiring. **Tomorrow will be soon enough...now I will eat and rest.**

She gazed with affection on her tiny friend, marveling at the perfection of the noble head, the minute scales on the back. How often she'd caressed those scales, large as dinner plates and shining with blue-green iridescence — now she could barely distinguish one from another. Yet he was perfect, a miniature Great One. A strange name for one so small. Perhaps she would have to think of him as the ordinary people did at home — as dragon. No, her people had always lived with the Great Ones and even small, he was Api'Naga. He would always be Great One to her.

She left the window, walked back to the food and ate another piece of the meat. As always she seemed to regain strength with each bite. She ate another and then tore off some of the bread. A full stomach would allow her to sleep. She turned, letting her eyes sweep the room and with it, the window. Again she was shocked at the growth those two pieces of meat had caused in Api'Naga. He was now almost the size of a robin from home. She frowned. He would be noticed by the old woman when she came in, even tucked behind the bars.

There was a raucous screeching sound and a large black-and-white bird landed on the window. Without thinking Kour'el raced to strike at the bars before it could begin pecking at her friend. The bird flew away and she stood trembling, turned now with her back to the wall. She did not want the Watcher to focus on the window or the creature there. As usual the wall felt cool on her back, but today it was not easing the soreness. Today her back was itching and she rubbed herself carefully. So itchy. Perhaps that meant the scars were healed. She rubbed again. Her shoulders were especially itchy. She kept rubbing.

— Are you all right? She asked, sending the thought. What if the bird returns?

There was amusement in the small voice in her head. **You forget, Kour'el, that we have talons too, but perhaps a blast of flame would be a better defense. I do feel much stronger...you could bring me some of the rock beside your moon to swallow, just in case.**

It took Kour'el some time to accomplish this. First she crossed to the pallet, pretended to rest, tossing and turning until her hands were underneath and could remove one of the pitcher shards. Then she sat up and crossed to the ewer and took a drink, spilling a little of the water so that her hands were wet. Then staring at the wall for a moment she moved over to the gray porous rock Api'Naga had indicated and began to scratch a crude crescent moon, being careful to catch the grains of limestone with her dampened fingers as they fell. At last, gazing at it as if satisfied with her design, she turned and went with uplifted hands to the window. There, while letting the soft breeze caress her upturned face, she rested her hands close to Api'Naga so that he could lick her fingers clean.

Thank you! She heard a tiny belch and it was all she could do to keep from laughing, not just because of the silly sound of it but from the sheer joy that things were at last so promising and from amazement that there could be joy at all in this place where she had suffered so much.

She ate some more of the bread. She would sleep now.

She was falling backwards twisting round and round

84

trying to free herself from the cloak wrapped about her. She was tangled in it, struggling to break loose, to stop her plummeting fall. She could see the rocks below rushing toward her. Above her the faces of people — soldiers and a woman with a face of terrible beauty. With a last desperate struggle, the cloak fell away and Kour'el was able to spread her wings, stop her plunging fall and swoop away.

There was amazement on the faces of the soldiers. Fury marred the beautiful face of the woman. Kour'el circled, dodging the spears and arrows some of the soldiers had now remembered to launch, then gathering her strength she pumped with her wings until she caught a thermal that sent her soaring away from the cliff lifting her back into the bright sunshine, high above the forest she'd passed through a few hours before.

Kour'el wakened, sickened with despair. This was worse than the pain she suffered in the beginning or the hopelessness of her captivity. Now she knew why her back ached as if torn apart. Now she knew what she had lost and it was unbearable. She lay on the pallet trembling, her eyes squeezed shut to hold back the tears.

Poor Kour'el...poor broken bird. The sending was tentative, so filled with an emotion Kour'el was not used to receiving from her great friend, that she could hold back no longer. Kour'el wept.

CHAPTER SIXTEEN

To spare the donkeys, Brede walked beside the cart and from time to time Petaurus did so as well. At first he had only been able to do so for short periods. But as he regained his strength he was able to walk longer and longer.

As they neared the city, the poverty of the villagers shocked both of them but especially the younger man who had lived all his life in his own isolated village. They had chosen not to stay overnight in villages, not because of a lack in hospitality but because they had brought their own food so they would not be a burden to others.

This arrangement was safest although Petaurus realized that it might have been more pleasant for young Brede to have the company of people his own age and learn a little about life in the other villages. Still, Brede understood that it was not wise to risk questions. For the old man it was preferable. Years of solitary living had shaped his ways and he found crowds tiring.

He and Brede had slipped into a simple routine at sunset each day. They would find a spot near the road where the grass grew lush enough for the donkeys to have a good feed, unhitch them, light a fire and have their simple evening meal. It was the best time of all for Petaurus — a time when he could almost forget his sorrow at the loss of Maighdlin, the pressure of their task, even the weariness in his old bones. It was almost as if he was back in his hunting days, and the silent companion was the king; sharing the pleasure of simple food and the friendly light of a campfire.

"So, tell me about the market. How do we go about selling our wares?" Brede interrupted his reverie.

Petaurus concentrated on bringing the piece of cheese he held speared on a stick over the fire to just the right dripping golden color, then placing it on the slab of bread the baker had supplied for their journey. He was grateful that Brede was a patient young man, who'd grown used to the old man's long silences and deliberation when speaking. Actually he had been dreading this question. He had little experience with the market in the city having only walked through it on his way to the king. He had not been one of the common folk who gathered there. He had held a position so close to King Vassill that he was socially more privileged than even the perfumed courtiers whose job was mainly to amuse Queen Mariah and provide elegance at the fancy balls she loved.

This was something, however, that in his eagerness to be included in the trip he had neglected to explain to Brede. And since he had advanced the idea of the market, the young man had naturally assumed he knew about setting up a stall and arranging to sell goods. Petaurus had tried to fill this gap in his knowledge as best he could. He had talked to one or two old friends in the village before he left and so had some idea of how it was done.

"In the old days," he said, knowing that any error could be blamed on the changes wrought by the way the kingdom had fallen apart since King Vassill's illness, "people simply found a place and sold from their carts, or rented a stall from one of the other vendors who came regularly." He added as if in afterthought. "There was no fee but I fear the queen may have made it otherwise." He stopped himself from further comment. He had tried not to let his bitterness against Queen Mariah show, though the tax burden upon the villages was far more severe than it had ever been under the king.

⊱━◈━◦━○━◦━◈━⊰

It was not until the first light of dawn that the girls received their assignments. Maighdlin was looking forward to having a corner of her own, at least a pallet to lie upon, for the courtyard was too crowded to stretch out and what sleep the girls got had been in a tangle of legs and arms. She had not slept much anyway, in her concern for Mala. Now she was relieved that her friend seemed to be sleeping peacefully, the fever gone at last.

The people who came were representatives from different areas of the palace and, as the girls were herded toward the narrow passageway at the other end of the courtyard, each selected girls to work for them. By the look of those making the choices Maighdlin could not imagine that working for any of them would be easy. Even the portly woman in the apron, evidently the cook, looked eternally angry, as if having all the food she wanted to eat gave her not pleasure but dyspepsia.

Maighdlin and Marika stayed as long as they could beside the still sleeping Mala, but at last they were forced to rouse her and helped her walk between them. Several of the girls ahead of them were told "scullery" and it looked as if that might be the fate of everyone who came last.

88

When her turn came Maighdlin moved reluctantly forward.

"Let's see your hands," demanded one of the women. Maighdlin obeyed and the woman examined them, tracing the calluses on her fingers she had developed from spinning.

"Over there!" the woman said curtly. Marika soon followed her and Maighdlin hoped that Mala too might be chosen — at least as a spinster she would be allowed to sit. But Mala's hands showed no sign of a particular skill and she was directed to the cleaning group.

Suddenly there was a babble of angry voices, one rising above the others, and an imperious woman in a crisp white-and-black gown entered, pushing her way through, scanning the already sorted groups, prodding with her cane one and then another of the girls to indicate that they were chosen for the dubious honor of working for *her*. To Maighdlin's amazement, after close scrutiny Mala was selected, and as she passed the woman reached out and lifted her hair, as if its rarity was what had compensated for the girl's obvious weakness.

They were herded through the doorway opposite the one they had entered. Maighdlin strained backward, trying to catch a last glimpse of Talun, but he was gone. To her surprise the thought that she might never see him again seemed beyond bearing on top of all the other losses and hardships she had endured. His kindness and quiet strength had affected her more than she'd realized.

Head down to hide her tears, she followed Marika through a maze of corridors deep into the bowels of the palace.

CHAPTER SEVENTEEN

Kour'el awoke, the feeling of hopelessness washed over her.

The shadows in her cell were lengthening — it must be nearing sunset. Time to divide the last of the meat.

She smiled. "Feed the Dragon" was a phrase the ordinary people in her country used when they feasted and brought offerings to the mountains where the Great Ones lived. She had heard that in some distant places the people actually sacrificed their own kind to the dragons that lived there but the Great Ones of her land were benevolent and would take only offerings of the same food as that eaten by the people themselves. The people gave their best, and in return were protected and the land defended from enemies. Kour'el's kind lived in the high mountains with the Great Ones, honoring them. Some, like herself, were especially chosen to do their bidding. Most lived free as they drifted above the valleys and crags, beneath the sparkling peaks.

She remembered the dream. It was real. I can fly, she thought, as she placed pieces of meat on the windowledge. Could fly, she corrected fighting her sorrow. She wanted to see her back, her shoulders. What had happened to her?

I don't know. Api'naga's answer startled her. He'd heard her thoughts and assumed she'd been asking him. He was lying, coiled in the corner, too big to hide now but camouflaged by his stillness and the mottled stone he lay upon.

All I can see is that your wings are gone. And there are terrible scars on your back. True sympathy in his voice.

Kour'el felt a flood of surprise. The great ones usually showed no emotion except amusement at the foibles of her kind. But Api'Naga had always seemed to care for her, though she thought that it was just because she'd been trained by him in the service of the Great Ones.

"It is true," she sent, "I remember terrible pain and then.... Nothing. Then I was here and my back has been very sore until now. Now..." she turned, rubbing her back and shoulders against the rough stones, "...it itches."

Let me look, Api'Naga uncoiled so that his head was peering over the edge. **Hmmm...you've made it red with rubbing but yes...there are wing buds pushing through. You will grow another set of wings, I think. Remarkable! Yours is not such an inferior race after all!**

Kour'el wanted to laugh out loud. First with joy: she *would* fly again. Then with amusement. This was more like her old mentor. The Great Ones did believe that despite the ability to fly her people were vastly inferior. Mainly, she knew it was because, like humans, they could be killed, could die of old age or for other reasons. The Great Ones lived so long. Were they immortal? Until Api'Naga's death she had believed that they could not be destroyed for their bodies would reconstitute themselves.

That is not entirely true. Kour'el realized her thoughts had been read again. **Though it is true for my new beginning these last few days. But we *can* be destroyed. Sometimes when there has been great offense one of our kind is sentenced to die. Then because the body can be destroyed no other way, it is devoured by the rest. It is one of the reasons we grow so large. Ordinary food does not do that.**

Kour'el looked at him with horror. To cannibalize was one of the greatest taboos of her kind. That the Great Ones did this terrible thing shocked her beyond anything she had ever heard.

There was rumbling laughter in her head. **Do not be so appalled. Those pieces of meat you dropped... Why have I grown so quickly...? Think, Kour'el — we have been eating....**

Kour'el gasped. She had swallowed the last piece of meat before she walked to the window. Now that she knew what it was — who it was — she wanted to reach down her throat, pull it out and hurl it from her. She bent over, gagging.

Don't be foolish Kour'el. Whoever killed me knew that to destroy me I must be eaten. What better way to accomplish it? How else could you have survived such terrible injury...and regained your strength... You know your people are weak and die easily.

Kour'el stopped gagging. Awful as it was the Great One spoke truth. The Great Ones always did. Centuries of honor paid to them by her own kind fought with the taboo as she struggled to believe Api'Naga. — "But...you will never be as big...never be you again because I have...." Tears ran down her cheeks.

In a day or two I will be quite large enough to do what must be done to find a way to free you. And, the voice in her head was stern, and though not as strong as of old, it was a voice that would brook no disobedience, **...you and I will continue to eat the meat that is brought. You need those wings!**

There was a flapping, scrambling, screeching sound and the black-and-white bird landed and seized the last piece of meat. Instantly a flash of flame sent it flying away from the ledge. Api'Naga was now nearly as big as the bird itself, bigger if you counted the length of his tail.

Kour'el's heart sank. Surely the Watcher would have seen that. She could only hope that whoever it was would assume there had been two birds on the ledge and the flash was merely part of the orange brilliance of the setting sun.

She hurried to scratch some more grains from the stone while it was still light. If he were discovered, Api'Naga would need the power to fly away.

Chapter Eighteen

Maighdlin's hopes of a chance to rest before she began work were shattered. They were taken to a large room filled with spinning wheels. There were a few girls already there, their faces pale and drawn as though it had been months since they had seen the sun. They were thin too and the bony arms protruding from their ragged sleeves made her wonder what food they were given. Luckily there were more wheels than girls to work them and she was able to choose one very similar to the one at home. She wanted to prove that she could do a good job, for she was quite sure anyone who didn't would soon be moved to scrubbing, either pots in the scullery or the acres of stone floors that seemed to go on forever in the palace.

All the new girls were handed baskets of wool. Maighdlin looked at hers with dismay. Obviously it had not been teased or carded — it was full of bits of straw and dirt. There seemed to be no one in charge although a soldier stood at the only door. Maighdlin had spotted some large baskets at the edge of the room as they entered. Now might be a good time to check for carders. She rose quickly and found two pairs of the flat boards embedded with bent wire. Most of them had broken handles but the four she picked were in relatively good condition. She walked quickly back to her place and as she passed Marika she handed her the extra set.

She knew the soldier at the doorway had watched every move she made but either such movement about the room was allowed or she had done it with such confidence that he assumed she had been granted permission to do it. She thought perhaps it was the latter since the girl next to her stopped staring listlessly at her wheel and stared at Maighdlin in wonder. Maighdlin smiled. She had noticed that the girl was attempting to spin the wool even in its dirty condition. She held out the carders.

"Do you want to use these first? I won't need them until I've teased some of the dirt and bits of straw out." She suited actions to words as she began to pull the wool apart, back and forth in her hands, "teasing" it until the foreign material fell out.

The girl next to her looked amazed to have been spoken to. A little color came into her cheeks. She spoke softly, almost a whisper as she took the offering. "Thank you."

Maighdlin took the opportunity while brushing off her skirt to observe the room more closely. Even with the newcomers there were not many more than a dozen girls and women seated at the wheels. The woman who had chosen them and brought them here was nowhere to be seen. The soldier was slumped against the door frame looking extremely bored.

She realized that she had not eaten since the partly roasted, partly burned potato the night before last.

"I'm starving," she said to the girl beside her, "when do we get to eat around here?"

She realized as she spoke that her words were ill-chosen, even cruel, for a bitter smile twisted the girl's thin face.

"Tonight," was the reply, "if we are lucky, if we have worked well and if there is any food left in the kitchens we will be given some scraps." The girl gave her a hopeless look. "Do not count on it."

Maighdlin shook her head. "I'm sorry..." she said, "I didn't know."

The girl smiled then. "Nobody does when they first come here. I am Tara, by the way..." and before Maighdlin could ask added, "...it has been nearly a year since I was taken from my village."

Maighdlin tried to hide her shock. The girl looked much too old to have been included if she had been here less than a year — could it be that palace life aged one so? "I am Maighdlin," she said quickly. "Five days ago I was in my home...." She stopped, realizing she was close to tears. "Here," she said quickly pushing the now clean basket of wool toward the girl. "Let me clean your wool and you can card mine." She had noticed that although the girl had not bothered to clean the wool before she began, she handled the carders expertly, pulling the wool into long smooth strands and removing the flat rectangular clumps to place beneath her wheel ready to be spun.

Maighdlin looked around and noticed that Marika had worked out a similar arrangement of sharing the carders with an older woman beside her. In fact as she watched Marika had moved over and was showing a younger girl nearby how to tease the wool to clean it. She smiled at her approvingly. Good! If their food supply was based on the quality and quantity of the work produced, it would pay to work together.

At last she finished the teasing and carding and could begin to spin. There was something so relaxing and pleasant about spinning that in spite of the hunger gnawing at her Maighdlin began to hum contentedly as her foot worked the treadle keeping the wheel turning, the wool twisting into yarn that slipped smoothly between her fingers to wind onto the spindle. Almost without thinking the hum became words of an old spinning song her mother had taught her. "...noisily whirring...spins the wheel..." she sang softly. She hadn't realized she was singing out loud until she heard Marika join in, and then one or two others. "...swings the wheel, while the foot's stirring..." Soon Tara and the rest joined until nearly everyone was singing.

The soldier drowsing against the door frame jerked awake and looked at them with an expression of such amazement that Maighdlin almost laughed out loud. At that moment the woman who'd brought them walked in the door. Her look of shock was mixed with anger as she stared around the room and the singers quieted instantly. Maighdlin tensed for scolding or worse as the woman began to pace between the rows, but as she progressed there seemed to be less annoyance in her walk. She bent to look at the skeins of wool Marika had produced and Maighdlin felt that she was holding back words of praise. Her expression had changed to one of pleased amazement. She seated herself at a long table at the front of the room and the spinners began to carry their finished yarn to her. Soon the table was heaped with skeins.

"If production has anything to do with it," Maighdlin murmured to Tara, "we will eat tonight."

➤┄◆➤┄O┄◈┄◆┄┄

Petaurus was more shocked than Maighdlin had been at the terrible conditions in the market square. He had tried

97

to prepare himself for a change but he could never have imagined the squalor of it. He set about finding a place for their cart and they had barely unhitched the donkeys when a surly man claiming to be the queen's tax collector came by.

"Rent for the space — pay up!" he demanded loudly.

"But we've sold nothing yet," said Petaurus reasonably.

"We can pay you later, when we've made some money or...." He had been about to suggest that they could pay in produce when the man seized one of the sacks of grain and threw it over his shoulder.

"This will serve for now," he said as he disappeared in the crowd.

Petaurus looked around. To his amazement he noticed someone familiar walking through the crowd. Someone he'd known long ago, now older and bent as he was, making it difficult to place the man. Yes! That was it — he remembered. Could this be Tautarus, Captain of the King's Guard? If it was, he had fallen on hard times indeed. He turned to Brede who was obviously having difficulty with the appalling stench of the market. "Why don't you move about and see what you can see. Be careful that you don't stray where you will be thought out of place." In other words, Petaurus said with a look, don't go too near the palace.

Brede nodded and moved away through the crowd.

It *was* Tautarus he realized as the man neared. Ah! There was recognition in the man's eyes — he knew the former huntsman as well. Both had changed greatly, but with Tautarus it was not just aging. His beard was unkempt, his clothes tattered and he was thin, almost emaciated — only a few steps from being one of the beggars lying listlessly not far from them.

Petaurus said nothing. He reached into the basket under the seat of the cart and broke off a hunk of bread which he handed to his old friend. The food was seized and quickly devoured, the flask of watered wine that followed drained by several inches in one long draught. Only then did Tautarus nod and reach out his hand in greeting. The two of them leaned against the cart, carefully surveying the crowd. Still not a word had passed between them. At last Petaurus spoke.

"I did not know things were *this* bad in the city."

Tautarus again scrutinized the people closest to them before he replied. "Worse each day. He has not been seen for many months." He bent as if brushing something from his filthy boot. "She rules entirely.... It is said there is not even a pretense now of consulting him. Some of us wonder..." he straightened again and spoke as if to himself, "...if he is still alive." Then he spoke directly in a louder voice. "And so what brings you to the city?"

Petaurus shook his head sadly. "My granddaughter is one of those taken in the last batch of palace slaves." He was glad that his friend only nodded, expressing no surprise at the unspoken assumption that he was here to rescue her. He could not keep the pleading from his voice. "What is the situation there?" He knew his friend would read all the other requests in that question: Do you know anyone working there? Is there a way in? Are the servants ever seen outside?

Quietly the two men crouched beside the cart sharing the bread and wine and Tautarus was still speaking softly when Brede returned several hours later.

CHAPTER NINETEEN

———··———

The black-and-white bird returned the next day. Kour'el was shocked at how much bigger it had grown. Api'Naga would be bigger too, too big to hide on the windowledge now. Where was he? She shooed the bird from the window. Perhaps her friend was clinging to the stones outside the window. Perhaps there was a ledge below that had been invisible when she looked out.

She felt an overwhelming loneliness. The sun's rays had almost reached the mark above the stand, but she had to risk dragging it across to the window in the hope of finding him outside.

— Api'Naga, where are you? she thought miserably as she began to tug on it.

I am here! Hiding behind the stand. Don't move it!

Kour'el hoped her gasp had not been heard. She lowered the stand as if it had been too heavy for her. She'd seen him — he was as big as the black-and-white bird now. No wonder he had left the window. Another thought occurred to her.

— Before you eat today you will have to squeeze back out the window, or you will grow too large and be trapped in here as I am, she sent.

She was conscious of something in Api'Naga's voice she'd never heard before — could it be embarrassment? **You are right. I went out to fly around your prison and when I** returned I was so tired, I could only think to hide. The voice did sound tired.

Kour'el had turned and stood facing the window in order to distract the Watcher. She must return to her pallet — she was always sitting on the pallet when the woman came — but she wanted to know what Api'Naga had learned.

You are at the top of a stone tower, surrounded by a stone fence which stands on a cliff. Fortunately there was moonlight and I could see. There is no door visible at the foot of the tower. I could not see how your old woman enters. I did not see more. I was attacked by an owl and had to use flame to escape.

Kour'el turned back. The sun was nearly to the mark now but she must hear the rest.

There was not enough power left then to fly as high as the tower window. So I crawled up the wall and did not reach the top until nearly dawn. I wanted to hide before your Watcher could see me. She could sense his exhaustion and knew he was finished.

When the old woman came a few moments later, Kour'el was seated cross-legged as always on her pallet. How did the woman enter? Api'Naga had not mentioned if there were other windows or if hers was the only one. There might be a tunnel underneath.

More than that Kour'el wondered something else. If she could read the dragon's thoughts perhaps she could read those of the old woman, and learn from them. She hoped that in her curiosity she was not staring at the old woman more than usual. But the woman seemed to be staring at her longer too. Difficult to tell beneath the hood. And no matter how she tried she could not penetrate the old woman's thinking. Now Kour'el feared she had offended.

Was the curtsy stiffer — more forced? There seemed to be an impertinence in the old woman's manner that Kour'el had not noticed before.

When the woman was gone Kour'el tried to behave as she always did. She drank the broth, ate the vegetables and sorted out the pieces of meat. She knew she must eat a few as usual but she resisted. Now that she knew....

Eat! There was no mistaking the command in Api'Naga's message.

All her old training came back. The Great One must be obeyed. She picked up a piece and chewed slowly, trying to concentrate on the strength she seemed to gain even before she swallowed. Could she swallow? She felt her throat tighten.

Eat!

Training took over. There was no resisting an order from Api'Naga. She swallowed. The next piece was easier, and the next. As always she felt instantly stronger. That made her curious.

— Why, she sent, do I not grow larger as you and the bird did? I know I am stronger but I am no bigger than I was before.

There is no doubt that your kind do seem to lack some abilities. I would have thought the meat of the dragon would affect all creatures the same. It is the human in you, I suppose. But you are growing...at least one part of you is!

Kour'el reached as far as she could over her shoulder. She could feel them now. Her wings were more than sprouts. She wished she had something to cover them with, to hide them but the simple garment she wore had no back. It tied at the neck, covered only her breasts and fell softly as a layered skirt.

Useless, she thought, the Watcher would have seen them before she did. How long did she have before they were fully grown? Two or three days perhaps at this rate. Good. If she and Api'Naga had to separate then let it be for as short a time as possible.

She regretted that she could not feed him until nightfall when he could get to the window. But there was something she could do. She seized the stone shard. The Watcher had seen her carving so she had not bothered to hide it. She began to scratch at the rock, enlarging the crescent she had made before, noticing with satisfaction that the granules of stone that sifted down were falling behind the stand to Api'Naga. She worked with determination, adding other phases of the moon until there were a series of shapes. She worked until her hands were blistered and sore from holding the sharp bit of stone, and many grains of limestone had fallen. She worked until a voice in her head said **Enough! Leave something of the wall.**

Then she stopped, picked up a piece of meat and walked to the window holding it like an offering in her upraised hands as she'd done the day before. This time though she did not place it on the ledge but in her mouth. Now that her wings showed she knew she must grow them as quickly as possible. Food and rest were what was needed. All else she could leave to Api'Naga.

She found she could not lie on her back at all now; before she'd thought it was because of the pain, now she knew that her kind always lay curled on either side, the way she preferred. She was conscious that her wings had grown large enough to fold, the gossamer feel of them against her skin like a caress. How could she have forgotten that feeling?

She lay thinking. Maybe they should just keep Api'Naga inside until he was large enough to overpower the old woman and let them escape by the door. No. The thought of them both imprisoned here was too much. Besides she'd sensed there was more to the old woman today than she'd first thought. There was power there. Perhaps the old woman was not what she seemed.

Soon the sun's rays had warmed the room enough that she felt drowsy, and she slept.

She felt glorious and free, soaring high above the tree-tops and she wanted to stay there, dipping and gliding, relieved to be free of the cloak, the terrible confinement she'd felt in falling. But she knew she must hide, must warn Api'Naga. Even now it might be too late. The wall behind her was open and soldiers were pouring down the path. She dove for the trees, startling a flock of pink and grey parrots that broke and swooped away. The tree canopy was thick and below, the trunks too close together for more than brief fluttering flight. She would have to run. And she knew the soldiers would have marked the place of her descent and be on their way. She would never make it back to where Api'Naga rested. It was late in the day. All she could do was hide in the trees until dark. She flew up to a thick branch that commanded a good view of the trail, folded her wings and lay still as death. If only Api'Naga did not try to come to her. She sent warnings but even as she did she knew that he was too far away to receive them.

CHAPTER TWENTY

Petaurus had sold two sacks of grain, several bundles of the herbs Marika's mother had sent and a few of the root vegetables they had brought. Even with the obvious scarcity of food, prices were hopelessly low. Yet though they looked longingly, it seemed no one could afford to buy the chickens. Still, he was satisfied with the day's work and greeted young Brede eagerly.

"Have you seen anything?"

Brede threw himself on the ground in the shade of the cart. "Nothing to help us, except the lay of the land. And what of you?" He nodded towards Tautarus who lay sleeping not far away, propped against the wall, content with his first good meal in many days.

Petaurus knew the "lay of the land." The city was like the wheel of a cart, each spoke a street leading to the palace, on a hill at the center. Narrow alleys connected each street. Even a stranger would be hard-pressed to get lost. You had only to find one of the wide streets. If you walked uphill you came to the palace, if you walked down you came to the city wall. Follow a wall and you would eventually come to the marketplace and gate.

He wondered how much he should tell Brede of what he had learned. He knew he could trust the young man's discretion but much of what had passed between the older men had been simple gossip and speculations. He decided to stick to the main facts. He moved around the cart, as if checking to see that it was in good repair, making sure there was no one crouching nearby who might overhear.

"My old friend," he said nodding toward the sleeping Tautarus, "was once Captain of the King's Guard. Now..." He let Brede draw his own conclusions and went on. "He stays here because he too has a loved one in the palace. His daughter, Lillia, started as a helper to the cook when servants were treated well and it was a good job to have. Now she cannot leave. But" — this was the best bit of information he had received — "once in a while she is sent down to the market to get food. Lillia is guarded but she sometimes manages to speak to him or give him a note...even if she can't, at least he sees that she still lives."

Brede could not hide the eagerness in his voice. "Perhaps we could give her a note..."

Petaurus nodded. "She has not been for some days...he is hopeful that she may come tomorrow."

He noticed that many of the venders with carts were preparing to leave before the queen's man could return and collect again. It seemed worthwhile to leave and camp outside the city, if not to avoid another tax then at least for the fresh air. If they went beyond the barren approach to the city they could camp where they had spent the night before. There had been lush grass for the donkeys and a sheltered spot. They could build a fire and roast a chicken since no one appeared to be buying them.

It did not take long for Brede to have the donkeys hitched. Petaurus noted with satisfaction that Tautarus roused himself and slipped through the city gates behind them just as they were being closed for the night.

There was food for Maighdlin and Marika that night; Tara had said scraps and that was what it was, though there were several loaves of bread, which the older woman who had sat beside Marika divided carefully among them. Still, the scraps were good and Maighdlin was ravenous.

"The queen must be feasting..." Tara said softly as she passed. "We are not often fed this well."

They were not given much time to eat but they wrapped what was left in pieces of cloth as they were herded out of the spinning room. All day Maighdlin had wondered where they would sleep. Now she was truly exhausted. She wondered how Mala had fared. Would they share a sleeping place or sleep with their workmates in separate places?

She searched among the guards they passed to see if Talun was amongst them but to her disappointment none of them looked familiar. Perhaps the troop of soldiers had gone to round up more young people in the villages.

They walked a great distance and to her disappointment she could see no difference between one corridor and another. She would never have been able to find her way back the way she had come. The place was a labyrinth of passages, each looking the same, some winding and some straight but all unremarkable. At last they came to a huge room. Hundreds and hundreds of pallets were neatly lined up on the stone floors. Some bore signs of ownership, a few meager possessions tucked beside though there was not much more than walking space between them. She and Marika were sent to a row that looked unused except for the one at the end, where it appeared someone was already sleeping. Someone whose vivid red hair showed above the thin cover. Mala!

Maighdlin rushed to her, afraid that her friend was not merely sleeping but terribly ill or worse. She was relieved to see that the noise of everyone's entry had wakened Mala and that she not only sat up and smiled but seemed to be much rested and probably in better shape that Maighdlin herself.

Maighdlin quickly claimed the thin lumpy mattress next to her friend and risked a few words she hoped would be drowned out in the noise of movement around her. "Where have they sent you? Are you all right? Did you get much rest?"

Mala laughed silently. "This hair may have got me caught but it's set me apart enough to be a maid in the queen's quarters. Not a treat, for she's known to be a tyrant to work for and there are beatings aplenty but at least it gave me an afternoon of rest. The woman in charge did not want me fainting away or doing any serving until she had a chance to clean me up."

Maighdlin noticed that Mala indeed looked washed and brushed and the robe that lay folded near her head was of better quality than the one she'd worn when she was taken.

"I have much to tell you. But we should wait until the lights are gone and everyone's asleep. I may not be sleeping here much longer. The queen's servants are not allowed to mingle with the rest who work here." Her voice dropped even lower. "It seems those who work for Mariah know too much!"

CHAPTER TWENTY-ONE

When Kour'el wakened it was already twilight. Still light enough to see clearly but the light was fading fast. She rose and walked over to the stand. Good. There was still over half the meat remaining. Enough that she could have one more piece while the Watcher could still see what she did. The rest must be for Api'Naga. She bent further pretending to peer in the pitcher, hoping to catch a glimpse of him behind the stand, but already it was too dark, too shadowy.

— Are you there? she sent.

Where else would I be?

The petulance in his message surprised her. Could it be that he was hungry and cross from his day without food? If so it would be a new experience for him. The Great Ones could go for long periods of time without eating — frequently food was eaten more for pleasure than necessity. It must be, she thought with amusement, that a growing dragon could be cranky just like any hungry young creature.

You are probably right. There was that unfamiliar tone of embarrassment again. **This is new to me — even as a baby dragon I was never this small — or this hungry!**

Kour'el smiled. The thought of Api'Naga as a baby was inconceivable. Even this size he was still Api'Naga. Weak but in command. How long since he had truly been a baby? Thousands of years? Millennia? Generations of Kour'el's people had come and gone — perhaps her people had not even existed. The Great Ones had been since time began.

It is dark enough now. Api'Naga was back to the old command. **Drag the stand to the window, I can use the shadows to creep along beneath.**

Kour'el obeyed. What would the Watcher think of this unusual move? She had never done this so near to nightfall. The room was nearly dark now. She could hear the soft scratching of his claws as Api'Naga scrambled up the wall to the window; smell the penetrating, slightly acrid, cinder-smell that came from him now that he was again capable of flame and flight. She raised a piece of meat in her hands, the offering pose, although she doubted she could be seen now. Then she brought the meat back to her mouth and ate, feeling her wings stir, her body gain strength.

She raised another piece of meat. Api'Naga had squeezed between the bars — a shadow shape on the outside ledge. She slipped the meat to him then brought her hands back to her mouth in a pretense of eating. Even though it was dark she would continue this charade for the Watcher's benefit. As the meat was eaten the shadow of Api-Naga grew larger before her eyes. She was sure he would be large as a condor now if he unfolded his wings.

Something swooped by the window. Was it a hunting owl seeking to seize the meat? Whatever it was it did not come too close and to her relief no flames issued from her friend.

She climbed unsteadily onto the bench. She wanted to unfurl her wings and stretch them. She needed to exercise and strengthen them. The urge was almost irresistible but she knew she must wait and do it later in the darkness by her pallet lest some bit of light from the window show what she was doing — and the Watcher learn the extent of their growth.

I think your wings are almost finished growing. You must risk practicing. When the time comes they must be strong. You must be ready to fly.

She said nothing. They both knew.

I am going now. Perhaps I missed an entry place, a doorway or window.

She wanted to tell him to be careful but his increased size seemed to have shifted their relationship back to what it had been when he was the teacher and commander and she the pupil, learning and obeying.

To her surprise the tone of the message that came was gentle, almost teasing. Different from the old one. **I will be fine!** There was a swoosh of wings as he uncoiled and lifted away from the ledge. She had been right. The shape of something as large or larger than the great condors rose above her. A silent shadow hovered in the moonless night and was gone.

She climbed awkwardly down from the stand resisting the urge to flap. Once in the darkness by her pallet she stretched her wings. It was a feeling of such relief and power that she wanted to laugh out loud. Flying was like that. Her kind often laughed as they flew with the sheer joy of it — joy in the peaceful beauty of the sky around them. How could she had forgotten it for so long? Had her memory somehow been lost with her wings?

And now, suddenly, she remembered the terrible battle that had taken place when Api'Naga had sought her out in the forest. Their trip had used much of his power and the closeness of the trees had kept him from being able to maneuver as the soldiers attacked with spears and swords.

Kour'el knew that as long as he did not rear up and expose his vulnerable underside he would be all right. But it looked as if he was going to be overpowered by sheer numbers. They were throwing nets, attempting to entangle his wings. Why, she wondered did he not engulf them in flame, had he none left after the long flight? At last he did. Not enough to do more than scorch a few of the attackers and send them scurrying back. But the stringy bark of the trees nearby caught and suddenly the branches and leaves ignited with a great woosh that seemed to suck the very air from her nostrils. She dropped from her hiding place though Api'Naga had commanded her to stay. Soon all the trees about them were burning like torches and they fled in one direction, the soldiers in another. The fire swept through the forest more quickly than she could have dreamed possible but luckily they found a clearing large enough for Api'Naga to use his wings and they lifted above the flames — choking and gasping through the smoke. She could sense Api'Naga was too weak to gain much height.

Go! I will meet you at the cliff! he commanded and she recognized the path and above it the stone wall she'd seen that afternoon.

She obeyed, her wings lifting her up, up to the wall and over, across the place where she'd fallen, past a tower, over the wall on the other side. Over a hillside with a sleeping village below.

And then a sound that filled her head, deafened her and sent her falling from the sky. The terrible sound that had haunted her waking and sleeping since that night. The sound she knew even as she fell to be the death cry of the Great One.

She was seized and dragged through a gate in the fence,

her head exploding with the sound so that when the closing gate caught a piece of her wing and tore it, she hardly noticed, so great was her pain. They dragged her to where a woman in regal robes stood watching triumphantly as the soldiers on the flaming hillside stabbed and hacked at the great body that writhed below. His dark coppery blood poured out like a flood, drenching the bushes so that they would not burn.

She had struggled, fought against her captors until the woman turned from her gloating death watch, pointed to Kour'el and gave an order. Then a sword fell and her own pain joined that of the Great One.

She stood in the dark room, clammy and drained of life, from the exertion of moving her wings or from the reliving of that dread night she didn't know. She dropped to the pallet. Again and again the events she had lost were replayed in her mind. At last she was able to rise and stumble to the window. Had she heard the swish of wings?

What has happened? Are you all right? There was no mistaking the concern.

"I have remembered the night...the night...." She could say no more.

Poor Kour'el, I think you may have suffered more than I did. The sound in your head must have been unbearable. I'm sorry.

Her eyes filled with tears at the thought that he should apologize for his own suffering.

I wish I had news but I seem to have found nothing. The tower has only one window...this one. When I flew very high I could see a city in the distance, crowned by a palace. Perhaps it is the one we were sent to find. If I do not return before daylight do not be concerned. Now sleep.

CHAPTER TWENTY-TWO

Exhausted though she was, Maighdlin was instantly awake when Mala whispered her name. Nearly all the torches that lit the windowless room were extinguished. Though it seemed that everyone was asleep, the room was far from silent. There was the sound of heavy exhausted breathing — even snoring, now and then broken by a moan and cry from someone in the throes of a nightmare. Even far from the guards at the doorway she could see that they were slumped over and hear them snoring loudly. She reached out and touched Mala's arm to show she was listening.

"Do you remember how you told me your GranDa hated the queen?"

Had she done that? She was sure she hadn't. It would not have been wise and he himself never expressed it so strongly. But it was implied and perhaps she had implied it to her friend. She felt her cheeks burning with shame. Such talk could have caused trouble had it reached the wrong ears. "He...he...never said it, but I guessed he did not like her...." she corrected.

"Well, he was wise. I was able to speak with another girl who was not well and had been kept back from serving... until the marks from her beating could heal. The queen does not spare the lash but does not want to see the results. She despises imperfection."

Maighdlin's heart sank. She feared for her friend. Not

that her friend was imperfect. She had a fresh young love-liness and grace of movement that was rare in the village. But she was impetuous and quick to anger at injustice, character traits that were bound to get her in trouble. "Did she tell you why she'd been punished?"

Mala slid her head off the pallet so as to be closer. "She said that she saw something strange." Mala's voice was so soft, Maighdlin herself could barely hear her. "It seems that each morning the queen disappears for an hour. At first people thought she was with the king. No one sees him — the queen and princesses wait upon him them-selves, and he is not there when the chambers are cleaned." Maighdlin was almost afraid to say it. She knew it was what her grandfather feared most. "Perhaps he is dead?"

"No, those who knew him say there are many signs that he lives. His favorite foods are still brought, his soiled garments are laundered... Anyway, this maid — Salena is her name — said that she saw the queen come into a room where she was cleaning. Salena was down on her knees try-ing to straighten a tapestry and must have been hidden by a bench. She didn't know whether to stay where she was or make some sound to show her presence so she hesitated, and when she stood up," Mala paused and gripped her friend's hand, "the queen was gone! Salena is sure she could not have left the room, for she would have had to pass by the place where Salena was hidden. When she fin-ished her dusting and moved to clean the room across the hall, she kept an eye on the doorway. An hour later an old woman came out of the room so Salena wanted to ask her what she had been doing there, and followed her right into the queen's own chamber! Of course she was punished."

"What of the old woman? Did she tell about the old

woman she'd followed?"

"No. She was afraid to say. The old woman had disappeared completely. But Salena does know the king lives for she could hear his voice protesting in the next room when the queen ordered him to sign something."

Maighdlin lay back. Near them a girl was screaming in her nightmare sleep and people were waking. Even the guards were roused and someone, the woman in charge of this place, she supposed, was moving along the rows of pallets toward them. They could talk no more tonight and she could only pray that Mala would still be allowed to sleep here another night.

>-+-+>-+-O-+<>-+-<

The queen's man was waiting as Petaurus and Brede drove in the gates in the morning. This time he said nothing, merely plucked the crate of chickens from the cart and walked away. The crate was less crowded than it had been the day before. Wisely they had left two chickens with a poor farmer near their camping place, one for the farmer and one for them to have later. Two they'd roasted over the campfire the night before. It had done Petaurus' heart good to see his old friend eat well. There was no doubt that Tautarus seemed to be stronger when they set out at daybreak, leaving him behind to follow later. They would stay apart this day to avoid arousing suspicion. But Tautarus carried two letters, one for Maighdlin and one for Marika — and enough cold chicken to see him through the day. They would meet again that night at the camping place.

Petaurus felt content that things were going as well as

could be expected. Today he planned to let Brede handle any selling while he watched the crowd to see if he could observe Tautarus and his daughter. The few sales they were making now seemed to be of the healing woman's herbs — and the bulk of these were selling to stall owners and others working in the market. Brede said it was mostly the sweet-smelling lavender and boronia — the heavy scent helped cover the stench of the market place. He noticed that Brede had opened a packet himself and was rubbing the dried flowers between his fingers.

Petaurus nodded in the warm sun. His sleep had been troubled last night. Sometime in the night, he'd been wakened by something passing overhead. Perhaps he'd only dreamed it — a shadow and the sound of wings that did not glide silently as the owl's did. And he had smelled the acrid odor of cinders mixed with a forest smell of pine though they were miles from any forest now. It was a smell that was vaguely familiar and it frightened him, though he could not have said why.

CHAPTER TWENTY-THREE

To her surprise Kour'el's sleep was untroubled by dreams. She wakened once while it was still dark to exercise her wings, then slept again. When she wakened this time the sun streamed in nearly to the mark.

The woman came, and left bread as well as the pitcher and water. She moved more briskly now, causing Kour'el to wonder if her previous stiffness had been a disguise.

Kour'el stared across at the food but did not rise to go to it. She knew the minute she rose to eat, the Watcher would see how much her wings had grown. Api'Naga had gone all day without eating, why couldn't she? She lay back down and closed her eyes, fighting the hunger that seeing the food had evoked. She would keep her wings hidden as long as possible for she feared that, even folded close in their mothish way, their growth would show. With her back to the wall, she would try to wait out the daylight. At last she slept.

Perhaps the exercising during the night had tired her more than she knew but she did not waken until the shadows were lengthening. Soon the sun would set and the room darken. She was ravenous, her throat parched. It was torture staring at the food and drink a few feet away. She endured as long as she could — it seemed hours but she knew by the light that it had probably been less than half an hour. Still it was noticeably darker. The sun was setting.

Soon. Soon.

Then she could stand it no longer. She crossed the room, seized the pitcher and without bothering with the broth, crammed her mouth with dripping pieces of meat. Still chewing, she drank great mouthfuls of the broth. To her horror her wings unfurled involuntarily. She was startled, and it was moments before she thought to fold them again. The Watcher would have seen that, she thought miserably. It was not dark enough to hide such a display.

You are probably right. You will have been seen.

Joy at Api'Naga's return overcame Kour'el's concern. She scooped the remaining meat into her hands and hurried to the window. As she did so the door burst open. She turned and saw two guards rush into the room followed by the woman, her dark hood thrown back now revealing a face not old at all but young and cruelly beautiful. A face Kour'el remembered all too well.

"Seize her!"

Kour'el only had time to flutter out of reach, her wings flapping painfully against the hard ceiling of the room.

Kour'el! Away from the window! Api'Naga commanded.

A burst of flame through the window sent the guards writhing on the floor and the woman retreating from the room.

Kour'el landed. She had nothing to fear from the men now but she could hear the sound of running feet and the woman's shouted commands. Moments later the room was filling with men, their swords drawn.

Fly Kour'el! Now!

She lifted, saw the flames had not only burned the guards but had melted the bars of her prison and she tucked her wings close and dove through, feeling the heat from the molten iron as she passed into freedom. Behind her the guards saw only a fearsome head appear at the window. Then another blast of flame filled the room.

Quickly, she soared into the rising moon, Api'Naga following. She knew where she was now and was soon over the wall and swooping down the cliff to the forest below. There was the barren place where dragon's blood had been spilled. Kour'el knew that no plant nor tree nor living thing would ever grow there again.

She spotted a sturdy tree and landed knowing that Api'Naga — still smaller than she — could land beside her. She was not sure how much of his strength remained. The flames he'd sent would not have been much for his old self but he was so much smaller.

I am fine. I found an outcropping of the rock and fed today. What of you? Are your wings strong enough? If they are we should fly on, be gone from here by daylight. It is the first place they will look.

Kour'el realized she still held the meat clasped between her hands, she opened them and held them out to him.

— Here, she sent, you must be starving.

I made a kill in the forest and have eaten one of the strange hopping creatures. It kept the hunger at bay, but you did well to bring this, it will help me grow more. There was amusement in the tone. **I would like to be as big as you are at least! And it will be the last we have unless we find the rest.**

He did not add, "of me" but she understood. Where did the woman keep him and why had that part of him not come to life again? Or could there be another Api'Naga growing somewhere?

You ask something that has been puzzling me as well. She knew that to destroy me I must be eaten. She must know much

of the Great Ones. We have a formidable enemy.

Kour'el stood perched on the branch. Slowly she flapped her wings. Api'Naga did not have to tell her it was time to leave. She could hear voices above them, behind the wall. Soon the wall would open and the guards would be combing the forest again. It was dark now but she knew they would be visible in the moonlight. Perhaps beyond the village they would be far enough from the tower wall that they could pass for hunting owls to the woman who might still be watching there. Kour'el hoped to see the city and the palace while it was still too dark to be observed.

They flew low, side by side, barely clearing the trees. Her wings were strong and she wanted to laugh with the joyous freedom of it but she held back. Once they were far enough from the tower they rose, flying high above the villages so that if anyone looked up they would see nothing but birdlike shadows against the moon.

They risked flying lower as they neared the city and the palace it contained but it was very late then and they hoped people slept. Even in the torchlight the amethysts around the palace gate glowed so that she knew that, at last, they had reached their goal. Api'Naga flew to a window near a large balcony above the main doors. Inside torches burned dimly and they could see the form of a sleeping man huddled on a low divan. His head was supported by mounds of pillows, his face lined by suffering. Kour'el wondered who he was.

I believe this is the one. The one we were sent to rescue — the king.

Kour'el felt a surge of annoyance. Just like the Great Ones to send her on assignment and not bother to tell her what it was. How did Api'Naga know?

Again her thoughts were read. **Truly, I was told no more than you were.** Her vexation obviously amused him. **But there was talk years ago of two others like you and me who were sent here and never returned. Oh, much rumor and speculation among some. Rumors and gossip to do with some evil that was taking over the land. Questions were not answered by those in charge. It was assumed they did not know. And now, you know as much as I do.**

He was obviously humoring her but she tried to keep from thinking her annoyance. She wished she could mask her thoughts and send only what she wanted to send. She'd like to think about the amazing fact that the Great Ones indulged in gossip just like common people but she scrubbed her mind of that speculation as quickly as it came. Think about what they must do. They needed a plan.

Yes. Api'Naga had kindly ignored the fleeting thoughts. **We do. First we must find a place to hide before daylight. And it must be not far from here for you must disguise yourself so that you can enter the city, even the palace, and see what you can learn. Unfortunately,** there was regret in his tone — **even as small as this I cannot be disguised.**

Kour'el did not try to hide her pleasure at the thought that, at least in this area, her kind were superior. She knew Api'Naga read her thoughts for she sensed the laughter in her head was not all her own.

As they flew above the palace it became obvious that Api'Naga had regretted too soon. High up, in a hidden courtyard enclosed by towers, there were statues of Great Ones. Dragons of all sizes coiled in all poses. In the darkness — for no torches burned here and they would have missed it as they flew were it not for the illumination of the moon — Api'Naga dropped among them. Here he could spend the day, a dragon in disguise.

Kour'el swooped away alone. Outside the palace walls, on a clothesline on a roof she found a cloak. She hoped the owner was wealthy enough not to miss it. She lifted again, soaring above the city to the countryside beyond.

Now she drifted, rejoicing in the feeling of flight — free at last. Her thoughts flew too. Back to the glimpse of the king. Api'Naga was just as confused as she was about their quest. They had been told so little. What was it the Great One had said? Something about a vessel. A ship? Api'Naga had heard something else, about "...two others." Had the others come with the same purpose? Why would they have needed a ship? She could think of no reason. No point in worrying about it now. She would think of tomorrow instead.

Below her she saw a spot not far from the road. A copse with a few trees large enough to hide her. A place she could sleep until daybreak. Then she would enter the city and blend into the crowd. She hoped she *could* blend into the crowd — a rather misshapen girl, her long hair tied back in the manner of the women of this place.

CHAPTER TWENTY-FOUR

Petaurus did not cook the other chicken that night. They would save that, he decided, for another time. They ate the last of the bread. It was getting stale and green mold spots showed here and there, but it was still nourishing and with hunks of cheese roasted golden over the flames and potatoes bursting from their charred skins when they pulled them from the coals, it was a filling meal. Knowing that they were not likely to sell much and more likely to lose most of what they had brought to the queen's rent collector made Petaurus feel less guilt about the produce the villagers had sent. He even permitted Brede to slip the donkeys a few handfuls of grain. It would be well to have them in good condition in case they had to leave the city quickly.

Tautarus had good news. He had spoken to his daughter, Lillia, given her the notes and received assurance that she would pass them on. Everyone knew that the new girls had arrived, it was a matter of listening to gossip and learning where the girls from that village had been placed. His daughter knew whom to trust and would be careful to risk neither herself nor Maighdlin and Marika. Even in the old days Petaurus knew that the palace had been a hotbed of intrigue — led by Queen Mariah and those close to her. But then the king had been able to stay aloof from it, and had refused to believe those who dared to tell him of rumors of darker doings. Petaurus too had, in his loyalty, refused to listen to what was whispered. But he wondered: if the king had heeded more than people knew why else take them near the tower on that terrible night?

It was late in the night and Brede was sleeping soundly. Petaurus was overwhelmed with weariness but he kept Tautarus awake as they reminisced by the fire. He had not told his friend of his experience the night before. He often mixed waking and sleeping as the old do, and he had lived so long alone. Before he began this trip his days had been so alike he would sometimes wonder, had Maighdlin come by that day, or had he dreamed she'd told him something? So he kept his friend awake, telling stories of the time just before the King's accident partly because they might mean something now, and partly because he hoped the strange creature would reappear. If it had not been a dream it might remind Tautarus of something too.

He smelled the creature before he sensed it flying above. Silently he pointed, watching his friend's face. But tonight was different. Two shapes flew above them. One he remembered from the night before, though it must be flying closer for it seemed larger, but the other was human, but with wings of incredible beauty — wings that shimmered in the moonlight. Involuntarily he touched the sleeve that hid the piece of gossamer that he carried to show the king.

He was sure from the involuntary gasp that Tautarus had recognized the shapes as well.

"You know them too?" he asked softly.

The other man nodded, "Once...the night before you and the king...." He paused. "We...the Guard was to have followed you and been ready by the tower if the king needed us, but the queen learned of it and countermanded the order. I did not know what to do. He had given an order but he had also ordered us to obey the queen at all times. Most of the men obeyed her but I went on, fearing the king had anticipated trouble and would need help. A mistake. He was not there to protect me from the fury of the queen."

He held out his hands. Petaurus had not noticed the old scars, half-hidden by his ragged sleeves but he recognized well enough the signs of a prisoner thought dangerous enough to be manacled day and night. He gave his friend a look of sympathy for the suffering that must have gone to make those scars.

Tautarus nodded. "On my way to the meeting place by the walled tower, I saw a winged human like that one. But when I arrived there were signs of a great battle and I was attacked and taken by the queen's men before I could see more."

Petaurus searched his memory. He had not realized the king had arranged for reinforcements — had thought the two of them were acting alone. But it made sense. Now he understood why the king had remained hopeful even after they had been attacked. He sat quietly deep in thought long after Tautarus' snores began.

⊱━◆━○━◆━⊰

Maighdlin had feared that Mala would not be beside her that night, but the disappointment at seeing the empty pallet was bitter anyway. Especially since she had such wonderful news to relate. She had destroyed the note Marika handed her as soon as she read it, dropping it into one of the charcoal burners that heated the long hallways. But the words were burned in her heart. GranDa was here in the city! GranDa and Brede! Marika had been passed the notes in a skein of wool by the woman she sat beside, hers from Brede and much longer than GranDa's simple words. But Maighdlin's note said enough — he was here and she should learn what she could about the king.

When it was time they could send a message back. In two days. She already knew something to tell GranDa, something of the king, thanks to Mala. Somehow she must contact Mala again. But for tonight her weariness and hunger had fallen away and she was comforted. Beside her Marika wept, as she did every night, but now Maighdlin knew it was for joy, not sorrow. She reached out to the older girl, saying nothing, letting the touch of hands say it all.

CHAPTER TWENTY-FIVE

Walking was not something Kour'el's kind did willingly. Her days of illness and confinement had made her easily tired. The copse where she had spent the night was as close to the city as she dared but still quite a distance. Now it seemed she had been walking a long time and the sun was warm and the cloak seemed to be getting heavier with each step. What she wouldn't give to be able to fling the cloak aside and lift laughing into the sky.

She couldn't, of course. She was relieved that the other people on the road seemed to take no notice of her, except for a few who looked curiously at her misshapen back. Most of them seemed to be making better time than she was. She stepped aside as a donkey cart carrying an old man moved up beside her on the road. The young man walking with the donkeys nodded a greeting.

Perhaps this was a good time to rest. She looked for a place to sit down then wearily lowered herself, trying to keep the cloak from clinging too closely and revealing the folded wing-shapes on her back. She would wait until the cart passed and she could have her part of the road to herself again.

"Would you like to ride?"

At first Kour'el did not realize that the man had spoken to her. Speech was something she was unused to: she understood but she was not sure she could speak a reply.

She should refuse anyway. It would not do to get too close to humans, even two that looked as harmless as these. Not that she feared them. She could read their thoughts, to her surprise. After her experience in the tower, she had thought these people's minds were closed to her. But now, Kour'el realized she would read any threatening idea before it could be put into action. These men thought only friendliness and concern for a young woman they thought was deformed.

A ride would get her safely to the city and besides she might learn something from their words or thoughts. She nodded. She would let them think she was mute.

The young man halted the donkeys and helped her climb up to the seat. She smiled gratefully and settled beside the old man. His beard and hair were white but she realized on closer examination that he was not as old as she had first assumed. He reached into a knapsack beside her and offered her a piece of fruit. It was unfamiliar but she watched as he removed the thick orange skin of it and she copied his movements. When she bit into it the sweet juice ran down her chin and she laughed with pleasure at the fresh taste of it.

"Do you plan to stay in the city long?" The old man's voice, like the tone of his thoughts, was kind.

Kour'el shook her head and shrugged pointing to her throat. The man seemed to understand and again she read sympathy in his thoughts. He lapsed into silence but his thoughts were rich. She could not follow all of them but she recognized there was a connection to the king. Kour'el could not believe her good fortune. But it was a young King — who was that? Not the broken man she had seen sleeping the night before. And there was a missing girl — his granddaughter. A prisoner? Was she confined as Kour'el had been? What was confusing was that she could not separate thoughts from memories. King Vassill in this man's thoughts was young and strong but then there were doubts as to whether he was still alive. And there was a woman, a cruel, controlling woman — the queen — Kour'el could have told him something of *her*.

Now the young man dropped back to walk on the other side of the cart from her. She read regret in his thoughts. Regret that she was there. There were questions he wanted to ask the old man and now he could not.

"Petaurus..." he began, and then stopped himself. He was concerned about a message — a girl dear to him. At last he decided he could say something Kour'el would not understand.

"Did he say when can we expect word?"

The old man took his time answering. He too was weighing what to say in Kour'el's presence. So there was a conspiracy. These men were not simply peasant folk bringing produce to the city market — they were here to help their women escape from the palace.

"In two days, if there are no problems with the messages."

With *getting* the messages to the girls, Kour'el realized. So there were people in the palace, who were resisting something. She wondered, was it the evil Api'Naga spoke of? Was it the queen?

The two men lapsed into silence. The sun was warm and the fragrance of roadside flowers drifted softly to her on the breeze. Kour'el might had been lulled to sleep but for the thoughts that were coming from the two men. The young man's were merely of the girl he loved. Thought pictures of a dark-haired young woman with laughing eyes. Marika. Marika walking toward him smiling in sunlight. Marika, her eyes soft and loving as they sat together in firelight. Marika laughing, singing, sighing. Kour'el smiled to herself. She would know this Marika if she ever set eyes on her.

The old man's thoughts were different and Kour'el soon forgot the smitten lover. Even in the warm sunshine she felt a chill. Not only had the old one seen their flight the night before, he had recognized them — had years before seen two creatures the same. Someone like her, a winged woman, had saved his life. Her wings tingled and fluttered on her back. It was all she could do to hold them still. He had once felt that softness, that strength. And then her heart nearly stopped for his hand had gone to touch the hem of the sleeve of his rough homespun shirt. He was carrying a piece of that translucence — her wing, the one that had been caught in the gate. And he wanted to take it to the king!

The young man had moved forward now and was walking beside the donkeys. The road became more crowded as they neared the city. She could see the city gates ahead. Once inside she would have no reason to stay with these two men and yet she knew they were perhaps her best chance. She was sure the old man could be trusted.

She waited for the next jolt of the cart to throw her closer, clutched his arm as if steadying herself and leaning toward him spoke softly.

"I have seen the king. I know where he lies."

Chapter Twenty-Six

Petaurus could not believe his ears. The young woman spoke but her speaking was not like anything he had heard before. It was as if the words were mingled with laughter. Her voice lilted, lifted, sang, though she had spoken very softly. He turned and stared, seeing her for the first time.

The pale skin, translucent as alabaster, he had dismissed as caused by whatever illness had given her the deformed back beneath the cloak. The fact that she walked with such difficulty had reinforced that impression. So did her obvious tiredness. Now he looked again and was startled by what he saw. Had he ever seen hair that color? Raven's-wing black yes, and she had pulled it back severely; but still the sunlight caught an iridescence like purple-green sparks waiting to fly forth if ever the hair floated free around her head. Where he had seen only weakness before he sensed a great strength. It was as if the deformed back, like the hair, was waiting somehow — waiting to spring.

But it was her words that set his mind reeling. The king — she had spoken of the king as if she read his mind. The thought chilled him. How could she know? Unless... Had the queen somehow learned he was coming to the city? It had not occurred to him that he could cause her concern. In the past she had shown only imperious amusement at his ineffectual attempts to reach the king. He had been so easy to turn away. Could Queen Mariah have sent this strange girl to try to learn why he was here? Even as his suspicions overwhelmed him Petaurus took comfort from the fact that the king was alive. Why would she lie about that? His fear was mixed with relief until he realized such news would be the very way to lure him into some trap. Of course. He wanted to believe King Vassill lived so that would be what Mariah would tell her spy to say.

He sat silent, torn apart by his thoughts. He would pretend not to have heard her. She had to wait so long for a reply, she might no longer expect one. The cart was going through the city gates now and the stench of the marketplace was a blow that sent the senses reeling. The guards at the gate were used to them now and despite the girl they were not challenged. One of them even nodded to Brede as they passed.

The donkeys knew exactly where to pull the cart and halted at their usual place without being told. But before Brede could come to her assistance the girl had leaped awkwardly from the cart and was being bumped and jostled as she moved away through the crowd. Petaurus stared after her with a heavy heart.

>-+-<>-O-<>-+-<

Maighdlin was seated at her spinning wheel confronted by the usual basket of wool. Today's seemed to have even more debris in it than usual. What had those sheep been doing? She did not mind spinning. The hum of the wheel, the feel of the yarn moving smoothly between her fingers, the clean smell of the oil in the wool combined to bring comfort and freed her mind to roam where it would, making the hours fly by. But pulling the wool apart to tease out the pieces of straw and dirt was slow, boring work.

Now though there was a break in the monotony. Someone had entered — two women followed by a guard. Did anyone get to go anywhere in this palace without being followed or led by guards? she wondered idly. But she recognized from their livery that these were not ordinary guards — they were the queen's own. Then her heart stopped. She recognized the second woman as they moved toward the table in front — a girl with golden-red hair. Mala!

Was Mala going to be transferred here? Maighdlin wished that there was an empty place beside her. But if Mala was to work here, it didn't matter where she sat. It meant she would return to the same sleeping room. They could talk. Mala would not have access to the royal chambers but that might be for the best. Maighdlin worried about her. She'd heard talk among the women who'd been here longest. Those who worked for the queen had a way of disappearing, they said. Rumor had it there were mysterious deaths. It would be a relief to have Mala away from such risks. Besides what good was it having someone there learning things she could tell GranDa if there was no way of getting the information?

The woman who had come in was speaking to the woman in charge. There seemed to be some agreement reached. Mala stood apart from them near the guard searching the spinners until she saw Maighdlin. Then her face lit up and she smiled triumphantly at her friend.

The woman who'd brought Mala moved between the wheels, stopping at last as their supervisor pointed to Maighdlin.

"You!" she said sharply. "You come with me!"

This was not what Maighdlin had expected. She looked around her. Beside her Tara's eyes were downcast. Something was wrong and it was not wise to question. All around, heads were bent to the wheels, no one dared look at her. Only Marika met her eyes with a look of helpless sympathy as she passed. But Mala seemed assured as she fell into step with Maighdlin. That gave her some comfort. They passed from the room and began to move down the long hallway.

The hallways were no longer such a mystery to Maighdlin. She had learned there were differences. She had memorized the only route she ever took and could have found her way back to their sleeping room. But they turned down a different hall that she'd noticed was the only one with torches burning on either side of the entry.

When Mala spoke at last, it was not to Maighdlin but to the woman walking ahead of her.

"Please ma'am, may I explain what has happened?" It was a humble voice, that barely resembled Mala's usual carefree tones.

"Briefly!" was the curt response.

"There was need of someone to work in the fabric room. All the materials for royal use are spun and woven and sewn separately," Mala spoke as if reciting a lesson. Maighdlin sensed she was choosing her words very carefully. "They needed someone who could spin and I told them about you."

Maighdlin realized that was all Mala dared say. Surely they would not have chosen her based on the recommendation of a maid who'd only worked in the royal apartments a short time? She realized that her supervisor had probably vouched for her ability as well. But why her? Was there more to this? She wondered if Mala had let slip that she had passed on the things she'd learned from Salena and someone wanted to have them both safely hidden.

She was glad she had passed her note to GranDa on to Marika that morning. At least he would have some information. And Marika would add that Maighdlin was now working in the royal quarters. Had it not been for the comfort of knowing that GranDa and Brede were nearby, hoping to rescue them, she would have despaired utterly.

They were climbing flights of stairs now. So many she began to be out of breath. Luckily the woman ordered the guard to halt for she could see that Mala was beginning to look faint. Obviously her friend had not fully recovered from the sunstroke and the long walk from their village.

Maighdlin's worry was momentarily quelled by her interest in where they were. They had climbed a long way and here, unlike the lower parts of the palace, the windows were low and large enough to see out. They were well above the city and the view was breathtaking. Countryside stretched in all directions, fading in the distance into forest and purple hills. Far below the road, filled with people and carts, wound through the barren space around the city. She hoped the woman leading them would not regain her breath too quickly and was disappointed to hear the command to move on. There were no more stairs but seemingly endless corridors wound around the edge of the palace. She caught glimpses at each window — wonderful vistas stretching out.

At last they turned so that the windows looked inward on courtyards built high above the rest of the palace. There were fountains and strange flowering trees she could not name and in one, statues of great winged beasts. Among them walked Queen Mariah and one of the princesses. She wished they could stop and have a better look but they were moving too quickly and she dared not slow down. A guard had fallen in behind them as they had entered the royal quarters. She dared not looked back but as they entered the workroom she stole a glance behind her and her heart stopped. Talun! And then he stopped outside the door with the other guard and she could not tell if he'd seen her or not.

CHAPTER TWENTY-SEVEN

At first Kour'el thought the old man had not understood her speech. She had never spoken before and she knew that her voice was not like theirs — her words seemed garbled even to her own ears. Then she read his thoughts and knew he understood what she had said and was wrestling with shock. When she had deemed him trustworthy, it had not occurred to her that he might not trust *her*. She felt with amazement his sudden recognition of her strangeness. And then as suspicions filled his mind she knew she had made a mistake. Why hadn't she realized this would be his response? It was natural for him to assume she was a spy, an agent of the queen. What else could she be? What else could he think? She wanted desperately to convince him of her good intentions but knew that her strange speech would only alarm him more and that there was no reason for him to believe her.

There was only one thing she could do. She must distance herself. Perhaps if he saw she was not lingering, trying to watch him, it would ease his suspicion. Perhaps then he might even think he had imagined her speaking at all. She waited until the cart stopped inside the gates, slipped down and disappeared in the crowd.

The crowd of people made her feel ill. She was used to the freedom of the air and the contact with other bodies was repugnant. Being pushed and jostled, feeling her wings crushed against her was unbearable. Then there was the smell. She was accustomed to fresh mountain air — the strongest odor in her experience was the smell of the Great Ones and to her that represented the comforting presence of Api'Naga. But the worst was the wave of thoughts and feelings, mostly fear, despair, and suspicion that now overwhelmed her mind.

She knew she could endure this no longer. Luckily she had instinctively walked uphill and the crowd was thinning now, and the scents were less obnoxious. Even so she felt weak and ill.

She managed to go further up the street and turned a corner, collapsing on a bench outside the iron gate of a house. Resting was good and the odors were bearable. She soon felt well enough to notice that there seemed to be some sort of fuss — a procession coming down the street. To her horror she realized that the person at the head of the procession must be the queen. Even from this distance the jeweled robes reflected in the sunlight.

Now Kour'el knew she must hide. The best place would have been back in the marketplace with the beggars — her misshapen back would have been a perfect excuse to join them. But she could not have borne the closeness, the terrible smell, the mental crush. She turned and backed down the alley nearest her. Even in her hesitation the procession had come nearer. She could clearly see the queen now and there was no doubt in her mind that the queen would soon recognize her. The cloak was a poor disguise. She kept backing up, not daring to draw attention to herself by turning and running away. The city folk obviously were accustomed to this sort of thing and were lining the street ready to kneel as the queen neared.

She glanced up and realized that it was too late to try to disappear around the corner. People were kneeling on the hard stones, if she stood any longer she would be obvious. Just as the queen crossed the opening of the alley, she dropped to her knees, covered her hair with her cloak and ducked her head behind the person in front of her.

She dared not look up and waited, trembling, expecting at any moment a hand on her shoulder, roughly pulling her to her feet, dragging her away — back to the tower.

It seemed hours not minutes before the shuffling sound around her told her the rest of the people were getting up and she was reassured enough to raise her head and make sure it was safe to stand again. Though she assumed the queen's progress would continue on one of the streets that radiated from the palace, she could not risk the possibility that they might return this way. Reluctantly she decided to venture further down the alley though it did not bring her any nearer to her goal.

Above her in the turreted palace Api'Naga posed motionless among the statues, a king lay helpless against the manipulations of his queen and a young woman named Marika was — where?

Now all she could do was find a hiding place and wait until dark when she could fly up to Api'Naga.

>─I─◆>─O─◆I─◄

It was lucky that Api'Naga had not chosen to hide himself among the dragons that lined the path or faced the fountain. All morning there had been movement about the courtyard. It began early with the arrival of the king, pushed in a rolling bed by two pages who then stood at hand to supply his needs. In the early morning sunshine he looked rested and more relaxed than he had when Api'Naga had observed his troubled sleep the night before. But even so he looked around from time to time as though puzzled — worried about something.

When Queen Mariah entered, leaving the guards that trailed her to wait at the gate, the king seemed to shrink back in an effort to hide himself. She saw him anyway and her shrill voice carried easily.

"What are you doing here?" Without pausing for an answer she strode over to him and confronted the frightened pages. "How dare you bring his Majesty to this place?" she screeched.

"It was my idea," the king interjected weakly. "I gave them an order."

"Orders!" She turned on him. Now there was an effort at softness but the persuasive tone was marred by a lingering edge, a rasp beneath the surface. "You know you are not well enough to give orders."

She gave the pages a look that would strike terror even into older, braver hearts and sent them scurrying back inside the palace walls. "Go!" She gave them a look that said "I will deal with you later!" Then she turned her attention back to the king. Again an attempt at softness of voice and manner that could fool no one.

"You must not come here, my dear." She began to push the king through the courtyard. "You know this place does not agree with you. And you know what happens when you deceive me." She reached forward to lift the brightly woven robe as if showing him his own legs.

The king looked and said nothing. His face was emotionless, resigned. The queen bent over him. The beautiful face smiled but the voice was a threat.

"Fourteen years ago you ventured where you should not..." her voice rose, "where you had promised me you *would not!*" Shrilly she spat out the words. "You broke your promise. What kind of man breaks a vow? Who can respect such a man?" Now she hissed in his ear. "The people would not respect such a king if they were told. Your daughters would abhor you, if I were to tell..."

She needed to speak no more. King Vassill had crumbled, his back heaved and he buried his face in his hands. "Forgive me..." The words were muffled.

Her voice was triumphant. "You are beholden to me..." she prompted, "...you would have died from that fall if not for me."

His voice was monotone as if reciting a hard lesson. "You saved my life...I owe you...everything."

Silently the queen wheeled him along. Then she stopped and her mood changed abruptly. Again she presented a smiling face as she stroked his beard and laughed flirtatiously, and her beauty was dazzling even to the dragon perched high above.

"Then you will keep to my wishes, won't you?" It was not really a question for there was warning in it.

Suddenly the queen paused and seemed confused, vexed at something once again.

"What is that smell?" She wrinkled her exquisite nose and frowned. "Is there a chimney, that smokes...I smell...what is it? Cinders? Something burning?"

The king lifted his head, as if relieved to no longer be the focus of her attention. He sniffed the morning air and frowned as if he was puzzled not at an unfamiliar smell but at how it came to be there. He looked long and hard at the statues around them, then as the guards the queen had summoned came to return him to his chamber, his eyes met those of the dragon above him. A dragon whose eye gleamed back at him, even though it was hidden in shadow among the other statues.

King Vassill allowed himself to be pushed from the daylight and said nothing.

PART TWO

Mala determined to spend a little more time in the sickroom if she could. She wanted to talk to Salena again. She knew if she held her breath and moved quickly she could bring herself close to fainting and since her skin was pale anyway she might successfully fool those in charge of the queen's servants.

It worked almost too well. The woman who'd kindly sent her to rest before now looked at her with impatience and mumbled, "Not one of those sickly ones...that won't do..." But she was taken to the sick room. Salena wasn't there. Mala pointed to the empty bed that she had occupied. "The girl that was here yesterday...?" she said looking around.

"Much better. She's moved...won't do to be talking and not resting," was the woman's annoyed response.

Two strikes against me, Mala thought. Sickliness and curiosity — I must be more careful. She bobbed a tired curtsy to the woman and lay down on the cot, closing her eyes until the woman left and the door closed.

She waited. There was a tapestry-covered doorway she'd noticed yesterday. Did that open onto an adjoining room? Perhaps Salena was there. Surely the woman would not return so soon. She slipped out of bed and silently tugged the heavy drapery aside enough to see in. The room appeared to be empty. She opened the tapestry more. There was Salena, in a chair beside a cot near the window — Mala was relieved to see how much better she looked.

When she saw Mala, she put her finger to her lips and beckoned her in. "Please don't tell anyone that I spoke to you yesterday..." she pleaded as Mala came close enough to hear her whisper. "There were many questions last night...apparently we were not to have been together...I think I convinced them I was too sick to have noticed you. I should be back to work tomorrow. Now go! Before someone hears us talking."

Mala vowed she would keep the secret and quickly left. She had just let the drapery fall when she heard voices. Someone was entering Salena's room. She recognized the voice of the woman who had brought her here.

"It was so kind of you to look in on the girl, your Majesty." The voice was wheedling. "She is much better today...she should be back to her regular work tomorrow."

The voice that responded made Mala's flesh crawl. She knew she should return to the cot but she stood paralyzed lest some sound betray her presence behind the tapestry. "We cannot be too careful...I have brought some salve. No, do not trouble yourself, it is better if I apply it."

Mala could hear Salena cry out and guessed that the queen's ministrations were none too gentle. She slipped back to the cot lest the women chose to leave through her room. To her relief the voices faded and all she could hear was Salena crying in pain. She dared not go to her while she was crying. What if the woman returned to tell her to be quiet? Or worse still, the queen decided to apply more salve.

At last the crying became moans so pitiful Mala could scarcely ignore them. Suddenly there was silence. Mala poured a cup of water from the pitcher she'd been left. If she was caught she would explain that she only meant to give the girl a drink to ease her suffering.

At first she thought the woman had given Salena a red

coverlet but as she neared she could see the girl was lying on the cot in a pool of blood — the sharp metallic smell of it filled her nostrils. She had never seen a dead person in her life but there was no mistaking the sight before her. Salena would never speak again to tell of what she had seen. Mala turned and fled back to the other room and the safety of the cot and lay there trembling.

CHAPTER ONE

Knowing that Brede was in the city — even far below in the crowded market — comforted Marika. She had feared that he might follow. His attack and injury on her behalf proved his bravery and love but it had been foolish too. Had he come alone she would have feared for his life. But Petaurus was old and wise and would not let him be foolhardy. For the first time since she had been taken she could let herself believe they might be together again.

It had been heartbreaking to have to destroy his letter. She wanted to carry it close to her heart for the rest of her life but she knew better than to risk such a thing. Not only her own life would be in danger but those who had passed the note — and Petaurus — and Brede. She had read it over and over, straining in the dark on her pallet until she knew each word by heart. Then she had torn it into tiny pieces and swallowed them one by one. There was some comfort in knowing that his words were inside her body, not just her mind.

Her own note in answer was short, she had no time nor place to write longer. She could only scratch a few words on a ragged bit of cloth with a charred stick. Maighdlin had managed better, having risked using some dye when she was sent to prepare some skeins of wool for weaving.

Now Marika carried the two pieces of cloth tucked inside her blouse until she could slip them to Gnelie, the woman who sat next to her. She was relieved when the older woman whispered, "I will send word that your friend is now in the royal quarters." Marika had been wondering how to add that information to her message with no writing equipment at hand.

Even the scrap of cloth with its smudged words brought joy to Brede that night as he studied it that night by the light of the campfire. He held the cloth to his face cherishing it. He knew that many people had carried it and kept it hidden on its way from Marika's hand to his but he ignored that, imagining it carried the scent of her. Long after the words had faded he would carry it. He looked across at the old man sitting wearily by the fire. The trip had told on him, though not as much as Brede had feared. It was good for both of them to be doing something and the knowledge that they could send messages gave them hope. He could see by Petaurus' face that he was worried about his granddaughter. Tautarus had not attempted to hide his concern from his friend as he relayed his daughter's message. Luckily today had been one of the times they had been able to speak.

"Will your daughter be able to pass messages to Maighdlin now?" It was a question Petaurus had been afraid to ask his friend before so great was his fear of what he was sure would be the answer.

Tautarus was slow to respond and when he did his voice was not hopeful. "I don't want to destroy your hopes completely..." he paused,"...there is a chance. She tells me that there are guards who move from place to place in the palace, who are not assigned directly to the queen but who come and go. It is possible that one of them might be...." His voice trailed off. "I should not raise your hopes too much."

"Then," Petaurus spoke slowly, "I must make an attempt to see the king. At least I know from Maighdlin's note that he lives." He had said nothing to the other two of his suspicions about the strange young woman who'd ridden on the cart with him the morning before. He was beginning to think he might have imagined that voice, those words.

Brede looked up, surprised. "But I thought you felt that would be foolishly risky... We know the girls live...."

Petaurus gave a tired laugh. "It's good to hear that you are the one now preaching reason. We've changed places in this venture — the young caution the old at last!" He sighed. "You are right, but we must do something. Soon we will have no excuse to stay." He gestured toward the nearly empty cart. "Not that we have sold so much, but the queen's "rent" has left us with little to show for our time at the market." He took a stick and rolled a few vegetables that had been cooking in the ashes toward the others. "These were too sorry-looking to sell, so we'd best eat them."

Tautarus gestured hopelessly. "If it were possible to get to the king, I would have got myself to him long ago."

Petaurus said nothing. Tomorrow he would search the city for the strange girl in the cloak. He rolled himself in his blanket and slept.

>-I-◆>-O-◆-I-◄

Maighdlin stood wearily in line waiting for some food. This was the only time she had been close to anyone all day. She'd been sent alone to dust and wash bric brac in one of the sitting rooms in the queen's apartments. The plan to have her spin had apparently been changed for she had spent all her time cleaning rooms in the royal quarters. And even more tiring than the work had been the sense of fear that seemed to permeate everything. She had not even seen Queen Mariah except for that brief glimpse through the window but her presence was everywhere. It was as if the walls watched and listened.

Now she craned her neck anxiously. Where was Mala? She so hoped they would be able to talk. There were so many people in the line-up and there were guards only at the far door where they had come in and at the kitchen at the other end where the food was being distributed. The servants covered for each other, coughing and clearing throats and shuffling their feet to cover the low rumble of conversation. It was in this way last night that Mala had been able to tell the story of Salena's terrible death. They were sure she had been killed because she had seen too much. There had been something in the queen's salve, some poison that had caused that agony. Salena had denied talking to Mala but did they believe her? Maighdlin couldn't keep the nagging thought away. Was Mala in danger too?

Then to her relief she spotted the familiar blaze of hair and soon Mala stood breathlessly beside her.

There was no denying that she was excited. "I've found it!" she said quietly turning to Maighdlin and brushing imaginary hair from her blouse. And then in an artificially loud voice in case anyone nearby was a spy, "I've got something in my eye, Maighdlin, do you think you could get it out?"

Maighdlin turned her so that she faced the light from the window. The ploy also turned her away from anyone in line who might be a spy for the queen reading her lips.

Mala spoke low and quickly as Maighdlin lifted her eyelid and pretended to peer into her eye.

"I was cleaning the room Salena had been in, the one where the queen disappeared and the old woman came out of...." The words tumbled out. "I guessed what bench she'd been behind so the queen didn't see her...she said she'd gone past that further into the room..."

Maighdlin made a fuss of taking a rag from her pocket, wetting it and pretending to daub at Mala's eye.

"I found it!" Mala's voice rose and Maighdlin shushed her quickly. "There is a tapestry of flying beasts and people and behind that..."

Maighdlin couldn't hold back. "Oh Mala...be careful...."

"It's all right, Maighdlin." She whispered. "I was pretending to clean behind it. If anyone had come in they would just have seen me dusting the wall the way we are supposed to."

"Anyone but the queen..." hissed Maighdlin. "She would have known." At home Mala's habit of acting without thinking had got them into scrapes and scoldings — here it could be fatal.

A flash of fear crossed Mala's face. Just as Maighdlin suspected she hadn't thought it out. Then the triumphant look returned. "But....you'll never guess... there was a panel... and a passage!"

It was Maighdlin's turn to forget consequences. "Where did it go?"

Mala looked at her and pushed her hand away. The line had begun to move, shuffling forward. The noise of feet would give them a few more moments to speak but they'd have to move with the others. Mala put her head down and mumbled, "A long way...I didn't dare follow it...I'm not as foolish as you think I am!" She grinned up at Maighdlin's serious face. "It just slants down a long way...probably underground. I'm sure it leads outside the palace...maybe even the city."

They were nearing the table where the food was being handed out. There would be no more talking. All noise had ceased except the clatter of spoons on bowls. There was stew tonight, more nourishing than their usual fare. There was even extra bread. One of the kitchen boys had taken a liking to Mala and slipped her an extra share — almost a small loaf — which they silently shared.

She should be angry with Mala for risking so much but all she could think of was that there was a passage and if it went outside the palace, outside the city... Not since GranDa's note had she felt such hope.

CHAPTER TWO

Never again, Kour'el decided, would she attempt to hide in the city. The hiding place she'd found, a musty little shed, was no worse than she'd expected but when she had emerged from it after dark, she found to her distress that the streets were far from deserted. No citizens, but patrols of guards moved up and down the streets. This was clearly a city where people were not permitted to move about freely after dark.

It did not take her long to learn the schedule of their movements, so the foot patrols would not have been a problem. It was the guards that lined the top of the city walls that kept her earthbound. They would immediately spot her if she flew up. Strange — she had not noticed them when she and Api'Naga had first come to the city.

At last she crouched on a rooftop. Waiting — hoping for something to distract the guards and let her slip over the palace walls. She hoped the courtyard where Api'Naga waited would be dark and deserted the way it had been last night.

The patrol passed by two more times and still Kour'el waited. Then from somewhere further down toward the marketplace there were shouts and running feet. She could see the guards on the wall leave their posts, crowding along the battlements to see what was happening. There were more shouts and the clash of swords. Kour'el gathered herself and lifted, her wings sweeping strongly. She dared not look back but swooped over the palace and dropped from sight in the darkness.

Api'Naga was moving slowly around the courtyard, stretching and flexing his wings as Kour'el joined him. It had been a long day and though he had learned many things he let her know that he now wondered at many more.

— So, sent Kour'el, reading his thoughts, you have seen the king.

The king, the queen, the princesses and a few courtiers, but mostly the queen, Api'Naga responded.

Kour'el could sense his concern. Confusion was something she was not used to in Api'Naga. She wondered what he had seen or heard.

It is hard to believe that this man could be the hero we were sent to contact. There seems to be nothing noble in him. The man I saw today is more deserving of pity than honor. And yet...

Again Kour'el felt his confusion.

...and yet, I'm sure he saw me and recognized that there was something... His eyes swept the courtyard, the shadowy statues in the darkness. **At sunset the queen returned alone and spent some time in that group of statues in the corner. I could not see without moving.**

He moved stiffly to an enclosed part of the courtyard. The statues of the Great Ones here loomed above them, more ominous in darkness — giant wings were spread and great bodies seemed to writhe. Though she could scarcely see it in the black night enfolding them, one in particular reminded Kour'el of a scene she had witnessed. The dying dragon. The death of Api'Naga. She moved closer as if bewitched.

Suddenly a torch shone in the entryway close by and a woman entered alone. Api'Naga froze and Kour'el had only a moment to shrink back, crouching behind one of the great statues, still as a statue herself.

There was no mistaking the woman who entered, though she wore neither the jeweled robes of the queen nor the heavy robe of the old woman who'd visited Kour'el each day. Now she was attired in gossamer that fluttered about her like a dying bird.

Kour'el felt a terrible pang of recognition. Her wings! Her severed wings, drooping in the torchlight. She willed herself to remain motionless but she could not stop the shudder that enveloped her body. She knew if she let it the remembered pain would overwhelm her.

It was Api'Naga who saved her. His thoughts flooded through her and curiosity replaced her anguish. He was using his closer vantage point to examine the wings. To Kour'el it had seemed that the queen wore them as one would a robe. But Api'Naga was sending different information. Somehow the wings had been attached, but instead of folding against her back, mothlike in repose as they did for Kour'el, they drooped, alternately fluttering and clinging. **Surely, she does not intend to fly!**

Kour'el shared the Great One's amazement. It was all she could do now to keep from peering around the statue. How did the woman expect to do that? Even with perfect wings it could not work — and these were missing a piece, the piece the old man kept in his sleeve hem.

Kour'el could see her now. The queen was climbing awkwardly onto a bench by the fountain. The wings flapped and clung and she slapped angrily at them. Even at this distance the pain was palpable. How could that be? Kour'el wondered.

Perhaps you only sense it because you see it, came Api'Naga's response. **Shut your eyes and see if you feel anything.**

Kour'el realized that was probably good advice. She was finding it more and more difficult to be still, watching the queen with *her* wings. If she could not see it would be less painful for her.

But what she heard next made her eyes fly open again with shock. A voice — the queen's — was mimicking one of the laughing flight songs of her people. She stood now, arms outstretched on the highest level of the fountain. Her voice had a harshness, a stridency in its tone instead of the pure joy that would have poured from Kour'el's own throat.

And then the queen lifted, fluttered — and fell.

So. Api'Naga's thoughts analyzed as always. **The queen wants your flight, not you.**

Immediately the queen picked herself up. If she had been hurt at all, her rage masked it. She tore viciously at the wings that enfolded her as if to rip them from her body. Kour'el shut her eyes and, to her relief, felt nothing. But the queen's next words proved Api'Naga was correct.

"I must have the winged girl," the queen snarled. "These wings are defective." She seized them and attempted to tear them away from her. Her actions were savage but the glistening wings' thistledown appearance belied their strength and although they stretched and snapped under the attack they did not tear.

She began to walk back toward them still muttering and ripping at the wings that clung to her. As she neared Api'Naga, she sniffed.

Kour'el held her breath. She sensed the alarm in Api'Naga and her own fear was great. Would the queen know the scent and recognize that the 'statue' nearest her was real?

"So dragon, you do not lose your scent even in death!" There was triumph in the harsh voice and to Kour'el's confusion, she did not even cast a second glance at Api'Naga. Instead she moved on with a cruel smile on her lips, though her angry actions did not cease until more torchlight beamed at the far entrance of the courtyard. Guards stood aside and Kour'el recognized the eldest princess rushing toward the queen.

"It is Father! He keeps begging me to bring him here."

The queen turned and her fury seemed to blaze from her, like one of Api'Naga's blasts of flame. The princess had come close enough now to see her mother and she stopped and began to back away. She had evidently encountered the queen's rages before because she soon turned and left as quickly as she had entered. The queen stormed after her.

Kour'el heaved a sigh of relief. She and Api'Naga were alone again. They would wait a short time and then fly from the palace.

CHAPTER THREE

When Petaurus and Brede entered the city the following morning the gates closed behind them. Petaurus looked around in alarm. What could this mean? The gates were kept open all day, guarded to be sure but people came and went as they wished. He had never seen the guards turn anyone away although they might be questioned if they were strangers, as he and Brede had been that first day. He saw that Tautarus had been one of the last group to pass through. He waited until he could signal his friend over.

"What is happening?"

Already his friend had been able to question some of the beggars nearest the gate.

"It seems that some of the citizens were demanding to see the king." He sighed and pointed to a new row of corpses hanging from the battlements. Four or five headless bodies dangled near one of the towers. "It happens every few months. Then..." he gestured toward the dead, "...*that* happens and people are afraid again...for a while."

"At least they died quickly — not like that poor fellow." Petaurus pointed to a man who'd been chained to a post on the city wall. Without food and water it would take days for him to die. No one could get by the guards to help him — nor would anyone dare. He shook his head. There had never been punishment like this in the old days when the king ruled.

"There is worse news yet." There was despair in Tautarus voice. "They say that one was not killed outright because he was carrying notes from the palace. He has not told how he got the message or who was meant to receive it. The queen hopes to break him by offering just enough water to keep him alive until he is so desperate he confesses."

Petaurus understood and shared his friend's fear. What if the messages had involved his daughter or Maighdlin and Marika? There was nothing to say. He gripped his friend's shoulder tightly, trying to give what comfort he could. Tautarus moved away quickly to hide his emotion.

"I think I will take a walk now." Petaurus mumbled to himself. Quickly he wrapped some bread and cheese in his knapsack and set out. He would spare Brede this new information until later.

It was the first time Petaurus had ventured beyond the marketplace and he saw that the changes that had taken place there had affected all of the city. Even when he reached the more prosperous streets closer to the palace the mood of the people he encountered was only of furtive despair and mistrust.

Now he walked toward the palace hoping that the strange girl, the queen's spy, was near. He had to find her. Whatever the risk, there was danger for the girls now. Even a trap might get him into the palace nearer the king.

He paused, leaning heavily on his stick — he knew the climb would be difficult and was glad he had brought the walking staff Brede made for him on their journey.

"Good day!" He smiled hopefully at a man hurrying toward him. Perhaps someone older — closer to his own generation — would be more apt to return his greeting.

Everyone else had simply looked at him with mistrust and hurried on by.

This time he received the same reaction, except the man eyed him ruefully as if this reminder of better days — when citizens could greet each other without suspicion — was almost more than he could bear. Petaurus sighed at yet another rejection but as the man brushed roughly by him, he spoke.

"Better find yourself a safe spot to cheer Queen Mariah, friend. It may take you some time to get to your knees."

By the time Petaurus recovered and turned, the man had moved into a side street and was waiting in a sunny spot against a wall. He had been right. Above them on the street, the great door of the palace was opening; trumpets sounded a fanfare and the queen's select guards were lining the street as if to keep the crowds in order. As he backed away, Petaurus wondered at this. Surely the people who moved automatically to fill the spaces and line the route were too lethargic to pose a threat to anyone. In the old days there had been joy and cheering at the sight of the king and queen when they moved through the city. Now there were well-rehearsed cheers led by people appearing at regular intervals in the crowd. Judging by their attire they were part of the queen's own retinue.

People were kneeling now and he recognized the wisdom of the other man's advice. Luckily he had ended up near a bench at the front of the building nearest him and he was able to use that to lower himself painfully to his knees.

He pulled his cap off and hoped that his clothing did not set him too much apart from the well-dressed people around him. There were a few like him scattered through the crowd — visitors to the city or workers who'd probably been caught on some errand.

He could see Queen Mariah clearly now. She was moving regally along, princesses trailing in her wake. He could see her eyes, darting everywhere, though the exquisite face remained immobile. It reminded him of the deadly calm of a snake before it strikes. And there was the same hypnotic effect. He wondered at the effort it took him to lower his gaze as he ducked lower, trying not to shift his weight to relieve the pain of his aching knees lest the movement draw the attention of those flashing eyes. The cheering rang falsely on his ears and his attempt to join in it stuck in his throat. He knew he must make some sort of noise. No doubt there were those in the crowd who would report any lack of enthusiasm.

To his relief they were soon past and he struggled to rise as the people around him pushed their way to the street to get on with their business. Many — perhaps the cheerleaders — had fallen in behind the procession and continued down the hill.

He felt a hand grasp his arm and hoist him to his feet. He turned expecting the uniform of a guard. Had he inadvertently committed some offence?

"So friend, I think you are a stranger here. Not familiar with the royal procession?"

Petaurus recognized the face of the man who'd spoken earlier. His relief made him bold.

"No..." He looked about them. The crowd was all but gone and the two of them stood alone not far from the palace gates. "I come from a far village, wanting to see the king."

There was no mistaking the bitter anger in the man's face. He made no attempt to mask it and Petaurus doubted it was false.

"It must be a far village indeed, and very out of touch," he said, biting his words. "Many wish to see the king — and die for the hope of it." Now his face twisted and Petaurus could read terrible pain. "As my son has just done."

Petaurus felt the anguish. One of the bodies on the wall. There was nothing anyone could say but he tried anyway. "I know it's no comfort but he died honorably, trying to help his people..."

"He died in vain!" The man's voice broke.

"Perhaps not." Petaurus looked thoughtfully at the great doors of the palace still swung wide, awaiting the return of the royal procession. "The gates do not seem to be guarded...is this usual?"

The man spoke bitterly, "Queen Mariah is confident that no one will enter. Not with the fate of those who tried still fresh in everyone's mind."

"Then someone should try now!" Petaurus straightened and began to walk firmly toward the palace. "At least then your son will not have died for nothing."

At the same moment, Maighdlin was being ushered along a corridor of the royal quarters that she had not seen before. Now what? The woman who supervised the maids had given everyone else the usual assignments and then told Maighdlin to follow her. She was hurrying and Maighdlin followed breathlessly, fearfully. Any change in routine was alarming. Even in the short time she'd been working in the royal apartments people had disappeared.

"You will clean the king's chamber today." The woman's voice was brisk but not unkind.

Maighdlin had found her to be fair though very strict and considered herself lucky to have been able perform well enough to avoid the woman's attention.

"Remember, the queen commands that no one speak to the king. Even if he speaks first." The woman looked at her thoughtfully as if measuring how much she should say. She added quietly. "The king...the king is confused and easily disturbed. That is why he is never left without the company of the queen or one of the princesses."

Maighdlin nodded. Her heart sank. If that was so then GranDa's dreams of reaching the king were doomed. She followed the woman into a large, sparsely furnished chamber. Unlike the rooms in the queen's apartments the walls were bare of tapestries and the floor was uncarpeted although the stones were swept. Even now a woman was scrubbing them near one of the doorways. On a raised dais was a simple bed where a pale old man reclined, his face marked with suffering. Was this King Vassill, GranDa's beloved king?

The woman ahead of her dropped a deep curtsy towards the royal bed and then another to the princess seated on a low chair nearby. Maighdlin stumbled a little but managed to follow the actions, holding her curtsy, but wobbling as she did. Finally the princess looked up. Maighdlin recognized her as the youngest of the three, Lurin. She had heard this princess was the closest to Queen Mariah in temperament — to the servants, that meant in temper. They called her the Firegirl, though Maighdlin did not know why.

When Lurin saw the two of them, she said crossly, "What do you want?" And without waiting for a reply, "Speak!"

The king looked up then too and Maighdlin saw to her

surprise that his eyes were clear and interested.

"Does it please your Highness that you and his Majesty remain here while the chamber is cleaned?"

The princess sneered and waved her hand toward the woman scrubbing the stone floor. "Obviously," she said scornfully. "Just do it quietly — and quickly!"

Maighdlin's companion backed hurriedly out of the room, leaving her to wonder where to begin. She racked her brain for protocol. She must remain facing the royal pair, never turning her back to them. That would be difficult. She sidled to the corner of the room nearest the door and began to work her way around, dusting the sconces and ledges and bric-a-brac. Luckily there was not much to dust. There were thalycine skins and heads on the walls, but surely she was not expected to do them. Nor could she reach the crossed swords and battle-axes that were fixed to the wall higher up. To her regret she had soon worked her way around and was nearly to the raised platform near the king's bed. At least, she thought ruefully, she would be finished quickly, as the princess commanded.

She realized that while Princess Lurin had gone back to her needlework, the king was watching her closely. The king did not look confused to her. Maighdlin decided that if the princess were to leave she would risk all and speak to the king — but there did not seem to be any hope of that. Then one of the balls of colored thread the princess was working with slipped from her lap and bounced across the floor towards Maighdlin. Without thinking she bent, picked it up and carried it back, rewinding it as she went. She dropped a curtsy and handed the neat, tightly wound ball back to the princess.

She expected no response and was backing her way to

where she had left off dusting when Princess Lurin called her. "That was well done. Now you can sort and wind these others for me." She pushed a basket of tangled floss towards Maighdlin with her foot. "Sit there."

Maighdlin sat on the edge of the dais. The basket was a riot of beautiful colors but her heart sank at the sight of it. Evidently Princess Lurin used a color and then threw it into the basket when it became at all tangled. The basket was nearly full and Maighdlin wondered when it has last been sorted. Patiently she began untangling as much as she could, winding it neatly and then beginning again. Despite the tangle, she worked quickly and efficiently. All the time she sensed the king's eyes on her.

At last he spoke. "And what village do you come from, maiden?"

Maighdlin's heart raced. She had been told not to speak to him even if he spoke, but how could she be rude to the king? GranDa's king? She tried to concentrate on the balls of yarn, as if she had not heard. She hung her head in misery.

This time the king spoke to the princess. There was an edge of annoyance. "Now the servants cannot speak to me. What is the danger of speaking to the maiden?" he asked bitterly, "I've noticed that I never see the same servant twice." He sighed. "Surely," he persisted, "There is no harm in knowing what part of the kingdom the girl comes from." He sighed again and spoke more to himself. "I *am* still king."

Maighdlin did not dare look up. Much as she wanted to see what her reaction would be, she was afraid to incur one of Princess Lurin's famed temper tantrums. Perhaps, if the king spoke to her again, she could point to her mouth and pretend to be mute. That was it! That would solve the problem. She would be disobeying no one and yet still not offend the king. But the princess spoke first.

"Very well," she said grudgingly. "What village do you come from, maiden?"

Clever Lurin! Now Maighdlin would not be answering the king but the princess. She dared not look at him — all her daring went into her reply.

"I come from the village of Blue Mountain, of the family of Petaurus."

She wished desperately that she was able to watch the king's face for his reaction but knew it was best that she did not draw the princess' attention to it. She was sure the king would recognize the name. She wished she could add, "and he is in the city even now," but she might already have gone too far.

"Aaah," said the king quietly. "I used to hunt in the forest near there."

And Maighdlin knew he had understood. She was filled with hope and fear of what he might say next. But he did not speak again. And when she dared look up again she saw that his eyes were closed though she was sure that he was only feigning sleep.

But Petaurus, only a few feet below, was truly asleep, though he had not meant to be.

He had entered the palace without a plan, seizing the moment that seemed to present itself. When he'd left the marketplace it had been to seek out the strange girl and see what she wanted, even if it meant falling into a trap. But when he'd slipped through the palace gates he knew that his first action must be to find a hiding place. Queen

Mariah and her retinue would be returning soon. There had been only two princesses in the procession with the queen, one was either sick or remained behind with the king.

If only there was some way of getting a message to him! But Petaurus knew of no one he could trust. It was up to him, and he had remembered the old armaments room — dusty and unused even in the days of the King Vassill's health. It was directly under the king's chamber — or what had been his chamber in the old days. Surely that would not have changed. There was a stairway, too, he remembered now — unused and partially blocked by rolls of moldering old carpets and tapestries. Often he and the king had taken this shortcut when they wished to leave unobserved — in those days few people knew of it.

Petaurus had moved surely through the corridors, avoiding the vast receiving hall as he had done so often in the past. Then he had avoided the courtiers because they seemed foppish and silly to him. Now he wished he had cultivated their acquaintance — there might have been one who was still loyal to the king, and that would be a great help to him now.

To his shock, when he entered the old armaments room at last it was obviously no longer abandoned. It was clear and tidy and filled with looms and spinning wheels, piles of wool and skeins of yarn. But most alarming of all, there was a vat of dye simmering over a few coals, indicating that someone would soon be back. Had anything else changed? He walked over to where the stairway had been. Now it was blocked by a large broken loom still covered with weaving. He had just slipped behind the loom when he heard the voices of girls and women. He climbed the first few steps though his legs ached now with the effort to hurry.

It took him a few minutes for his eyes to adjust to the dim light. He stood getting his breath back and realized that the purpose of the stairway too had changed. Before it had been the repository of unused carpets and tapestries. Now he could see that the lower steps had been cleared to store neatly stacked fleeces, ready for use. His heart sank — this meant that someone would be entering, might enter at any time. He risked the sound his boots would make on the rough stone steps in order to move higher up the stairs. There was a curve halfway up the stairway where it turned back upon itself. If he sat up there he would be hidden. If someone were to enter the stairway from the king's chamber at least King Vassill would learn of his presence and he would have partially achieved his goal anyway. He was comforted by the thought. Weary from his long climb he settled himself on the soft fleeces in the upper steps. If the royal quarters were still the same his king was only a few feet above him.

And then he slept.

CHAPTER FOUR

Kour'el was not in the city. Api'Naga had decided they could not risk daylight there. They flew to a forest far from the tower or the city, planning to remain there until it was dark again. Api'Naga killed another of the hopping animals and cooked it with a few flames so that he and Kour'el were no longer hungry. They would sleep until the next nightfall.

Kour'el was first to waken. She stretched her wings and then, though it was still twilight, she convinced herself it was safe to fly. Surely in such a remote place...and her new wings cried out to be used. She had missed the soaring joy of lifting up, up beyond the treetops in the sunlight. She even dared a flight song. Then she saw them.

A troop of soldiers were marching into the woods nearby. She dropped like a stone, hoping they had not seen her. Ideally, if the soldiers had not seen her, they would stop soon and camp for the night. Then she and Api'Naga could stay hidden until they could fly in the darkness. Still she landed near Api'Naga feeling utterly wretched. What if they had seen her and were able to gauge where she had entered the trees? It would not take them long to get here.

So, you have been seen. Api'Naga had wakened and was flexing his wings, stretching them as well as he could in their confined hiding place. There was no criticism in his tone, only a statement of fact.

"Perhaps," Kour'el responded miserably. "But...."

But we don't know. Api'Naga finished for her. **In that case we will make a point to fly away from the city. If we travel out over the sea until we are out of sight. That will be reported to the queen and perhaps she will believe that we are returning to our own land.**

Kour'el realized it was a good plan. In darkness they could return, flying high until they reached the city.

They flew deliberately low until they were sure they had been seen by the soldiers. Once the arrows began to fly, they soared high and turned to the course Api'Naga had suggested.

It was so good to be up here, though the darkness was gathering fast and Kour'el missed flying through sunlight, her song laughing in the brightness.

You may sing now. Api'Naga's tone was amused. There was a warmth in it that was new to Kour'el. **I enjoy your song, you know.**

This was news to Kour'el. She had always thought he only tolerated it because he knew it was difficult for her to stifle. She would try to analyze her feelings for the new Api'Naga the next time she was alone — when he was not there to read her thoughts.

I think it is dark enough for us to turn back to the city. Api'Naga kindly interrupted any thoughts that might be embarrassing to her. **We should pay a visit to that window and see how the king fares. We both know how ugly Queen Mariah's wrath can be.**

They flew high, confident that they would not be seen in the moonless night. They risked dropping only when they were over the dragon courtyard, hoping the darkness there extended to anyone watching in the restless city.

Kour'el was sure more guards patroled the streets than had been there the night before. Then they worked their way back, fluttering from tower to tower. The only risk came as they dropped down the front of the palace to the balcony room where the king had been. By keeping to the shadows they hoped they would not be noticed.

King Vassill slept as he had before but he was not alone. There were guards posted at the doorway and, on either side of the bed, a princess sat vigil.

Kour'el and Api'Naga settled in to wait. The eldest princess was nodding off.

I don't think the king sleeps, Api'Naga sent.

Kour'el looked more closely. She was sure she saw an eyelash flicker.

The other princess yawned. Surely they would be asleep soon. There were still the guards at the door though.

Just then the queen swept in. She wore the gossamer wings again, though her face and manner were more composed than the night before. She dismissed the guards, sent the princesses away and seated herself beside the bed.

"Do not think you can fool me by this pretended sleep. And I've sent those wretched guards away. How you continue to find people to do your bidding among those I've hand-picked, I do not know."

Kour'el saw the king's eyelid flicker but he did not respond.

Kour'el could see the queen's face. Once again, in spite of herself, she was dazzled by the beauty of the woman. Even in Api'Naga's thoughts she could sense involuntary admiration. But the harsh voice was a reminder of the evil inside that could not be masked by that perfect face.

"Another man dies because of your attempt." She

laughed now and Kour'el felt the chill of it. There was triumph too because this had drawn a response on the worn face of the king.

"You did not dare," he spoke with more pain than anger.

"I *dared* to kill a traitor," she hissed. "Did you really think anyone from the palace would be allowed to travel beyond the city and deliver a message? Are you still trying to contact that wretched cripple — your old huntsman? If you persist in betraying me in this matter, I will send to that village and have the man disposed of once and for all." She spoke musingly, as if to herself. "A fall, I think. It could be a fatal injury in one so old and decrepit."

The king's eyes snapped open and he faced her for the first time. Whatever reply he had intended was lost when he saw the wings wrapped about her.

"Where," he gasped, "did you get those?" Hesitantly his hand reached out, touched and clung to the wings — Kour'el's lost wings.

The queen's eyes narrowed. "Why do you ask?" Her voice was ice cold, slicing through the room to the watchers outside. Kour'el and Api'Naga froze. She pulled away from his touch and rose suddenly, going to the window to look out on the city. Her tone changed abruptly. "It has not been easy for me, you know." The voice whined piteously but Kour'el could see her face held no emotion, "ruling the kingdom, caring for you...." She breathed deeply of the night air as if to calm herself.

The king seemed to be gathering his strength to reply but he did not get the opportunity. The queen had not been calmed. She turned and screamed for the guards.

"Out there!" she pointed to the balcony, her voice quivering with rage. The guards poured through the doorway but they did not see the two shadows gliding silently around the corner of the palace.

When they left the king's window Kour'el and Api'Naga flew straight up above the palace. Kour'el craned her eyes to see what was taking place in the streets below. It seemed to her that the only activity was that of the guards patroling the streets. The marketplace near the city gates looked almost deserted. Her nose crinkled — the smell would still be there.

Api'Naga, whose eyes were better than hers, saw more and drew her attention to the bodies on the wall. **Those were not there before**, he mused. **Perhaps there has been an uprising. No, more likely these are just some of the servants who've offended the queen. Curious, though...that one is still alive.**

Kour'el looked. She had not noticed the man bound at the top of the battlements.

— Poor creature, she sent. Perhaps this is the king's messenger.

Then it would be worthwhile to find out what he was about. There was defiant amusement in Api'Naga's tone. **Would you like to give Queen Mariah something to worry about? There don't seem to be any guards near by. Of course,** there was amusement again, **they will see you as you swoop down but that will only serve to focus their attention and I can come low enough for you to communicate.**

Kour'el felt a surge of excitement. Api'Naga felt that it was time to act. She wondered how much his day of forced inactivity posing as a statue in the dragon courtyard had to do with it. She tried to think of other things before he could read the impertinence of her thoughts. Too late. To her relief there was nothing but amusement in his response. **I know that you find me slow to act but know too that the Great Ones consider your kind flighty...quick to act...slow to think. The reason we are teamed is that we complement each other. I am supposed to be the one who curbs your impulsiveness.** There was thoughtfulness now as he considered. **But your long illness and my...death...seem to have brought us more together. ...And I cannot say that I am sorry that this is so.**

Was there a note of embarrassment in this last thought, Kour'el wondered, that he had forgotten to hide from her? To save them both from this intimacy Kour'el dove to the prisoner. The man was in better condition than she expected. Bound as he was, he could not have defended himself from the flocks of ravenous birds, but the misfortune of those executed had been luck for him — the birds were busy elsewhere.

His reaction to her was not what she expected either. In her own land people considered the appearance of one of her kind a good omen — the winged ones came usually as messengers. They represented the Great Ones, the people's guardians.

But this man cringed, fearfully straining against his bonds. There was such terror in his eyes at the sight of her, Kour'el wanted to weep. Her people were known for their gentleness, their flight songs and joy — to provoke terror hurt her deeply.

Now what was she to do? She knew from her experience with Petaurus that even if she spoke, it might not reassure this poor man.

You'll have to try to free him. Api'Naga had come close

enough to send to her. **Some of the guards saw you descend and are going to be there soon. Can you undo his chains?**

Kour'el looked at the manacles. Judging by the ugly burn marks on his wrists and ankles, the chains had been welded to the poor wretch, and she could see no way of freeing him. She could hear the scrape of feet on the battlements above her so she gathered her wings to be ready for instant flight.

Not yet! Look above you. The chain there has just been looped over a peg out of reach. They counted on his weight to keep him in place.

Again Api'Naga was right. Kour'el could lift the man to free him — if his fear would allow him to co-operate. The scraping sound was louder. Looking up, she could see a guard descending — soon he would be at the ledge directly above them.

"Fear not. I come to help," she said slowly and as clearly as she could. The rippling sound of music dominated her voice but she could tell by the way the man ceased his struggles that he understood her. "You must let me free you. I need to lift you." She did not wait for signs that he understood, simply flew behind the prisoner, seized him under the arms and lifted him. It took all her strength and even then it might not work because the guard had arrived on the ledge and was seizing the man's feet as she pulled him up. It was too much weight, she would have to let go.

— Api'Naga!

What was she supposed to do? But then the chain cleared the hook and fell so that it struck the guard a heavy blow. He was falling, and for an instant Kour'el feared he would continue to cling to the prisoner and all three of them would be pulled over the edge. But the guard let go to make a grab for the pillar. Then she was flying, beating her wings with all her might to clear the walls and the other guards.

Again luck was with her. The guards that were aware of what was happening were engaged in climbing down the wall, and could not reach for their spears. Those down below had just begun to realize that arrows would be needed but by the time they could unleash their weapons she was high enough to be out of range.

Still her wings could not bear the weight of both man and chains for very long — her arms felt as if they were being pulled from their sockets.

— Api'Nag... she began again, desperately. But he was already beside her, heavy skin wings stronger than hers. Gratefully she dropped the man's weight across the Great One's back. Her only fear was that the man would struggle and slide off the smooth scales. Again luck was with them. Either from weakness at his ordeal or the shock of seeing the dragon, he hung senseless and did not move.

They were well above the city walls and moving into the country by now, although the noise of the guards followed them through the night a little longer. They would have to find a place to land soon. The old Api'Naga would have had no problem carrying such a burden all the way back home, but now he was only a little stronger than Kour'el. They would, she realized, have to rest and make the flight in laps across the sleeping countryside. Where?

I think we must go to the forest by your tower. They will never expect us to return there.

CHAPTER FIVE

Maighdlin had not finished winding yarn when the queen entered and sent her scurrying away. To her relief nothing was said about her presence — the king slept now, snoring gently. Maighdlin went to wait in line with Mala. This time they were both late and stood near the end closest the door and the guards, so they had only dared talk of how tired and hungry they were.

Maighdlin desperately wanted to tell Mala about her day working in the king's chamber, but even more she wanted to tell GranDa. If Mala had not pulled her out of the spinning room she would not have been able to give that small message to the king. But without the woman who had helped her and Marika pass on their notes, she couldn't tell GranDa, down in the marketplace, what she had done.

She was so wrapped up in these thoughts that Mala had to poke her twice in the side with her elbow before Maighdlin turned on her in annoyance. The angry words died on her lips when she looked in the direction of Mala's gaze. The guards had evidently changed shifts. Talun stood at the doorway!

She had not seen him since the day she'd been moved to the royal apartments to work, though each time a guard had passed she'd looked hopefully. Obviously Talun was not one of the regular members of the royal guard. But here he was. Did that mean that he was one of the people who were able to come and go in their work?

She was grateful that both she and Mala had been late arriving and were last in line. This time he could not fail to see her. It probably would not be safe to speak to him, not as long as the other guard stood there. But she dared to smile, though she tried to make it not too obvious that she was smiling at him and not just at something Mala might have said. When she glanced directly at him, he was looking at her and he quickly blinked his eyes to let her know he'd recognized her.

And then Mala did one of the crazy impulsive things that made Maighdlin wonder about her good sense — though she would be eternally grateful. Without any warning, Mala gave a whimpering cry and crumpled to the floor. Alarmed, Maighdlin bent over her. Was she still weak from the long trip? She really had not had time to recuperate, and the poor food and long days of work took their toll. Maighdlin's mind raced. If Mala were ailing, she would not be kept here to work any longer. What happened to servants who could no longer work? If rumors were true they did not live long. The queen did not want to support such people. Frantically she looked about for water, something to revive her friend. She stroked Mala's forehead and to her relief saw the flicker of eyelids.

"You!" It was a command from the senior guard. "Take that girl back to her night quarters."

Maighdlin did not realize who the order was for until Talun was beside her lifting Mala's limp body in his arms. She held onto Mala's hand and walked beside him. At any moment she expected to hear the order for her to return to her place in line but when she dared a look back, the guard who'd spoken had calmly returned to his place.

Her concern for Mala abated even more when she realized that the grip Mala had on her hand was much too strong to match the fainting pose. Just like Mala to do something like this. No thought that now they would miss their much-needed supper.

Talun had slowed down once they were out of sight of the other guard. Now he stopped completely and turned to her.

"Are you well enough treated?" His attention was all on Maighdlin. Had he realized that the girl he carried was not a serious concern?

Maighdlin nodded. "Well enough..." Then she decided to risk everything and trust him. "But...but I miss my friend back in the spinning room...I wish there was some way..."

There, she thought, I've given him an opening. If he doesn't want to help me make contact, he can just ignore the hint. If he does want to help, he can make the offer now. She did not allow herself to think of the third alternative — that he could not be trusted. That was not possible. He had always behaved with kindness and honor. She could not imagine him otherwise.

"I think I know who you mean — the older girl? The other one who was always with you on the walk?" He went on without waiting for an answer. "I've seen her, she seems to be well. Do you want me to tell her that you are all right?"

Maighdlin's throat felt dry. She would be asking him to take a terrible risk. Taking an unauthorized message from the queen's apartments to the rest of the palace was considered traitorous. But she was asking for more than a spoken message. She needed a note brought to Marika so that she could pass it on to eventually wind up with GranDa. Worse still, it would contain information about the king. She looked up into Talun's eyes — had she noticed before what a wonderful shade of brown they were?

"I...I would like to..." She couldn't do it. She couldn't ask him to risk his life, even though the message to GranDa would be vitally important. And she couldn't tell him how important it was without involving him. She lowered her eyes feeling utterly miserable. "Never mind...just tell her I am fine."

He seemed to pale beneath his tan, then braced himself and began walking. Now he spoke without looking at her. "You want to give me a written message."

It was a statement, not a question. Maighdlin nodded. She could feel his tension as well as her own. Messengers were killed. She wanted to cry and apologize for even thinking of such a thing. He walked beside her, carrying Mala as if she weighed nothing. They were nearing the sleeping room — only two more turns of the corridor.

When he spoke again it was so soft she could barely hear. "It is important to you?"

Again she nodded. She wanted to tell him about GranDa here in the city, about the king, about everything but the less he knew, the less his danger would be and she bit her tongue until the pain made her head ache.

"Write it quickly then."

She knew he heard her surprised gasp and her whispered, "Thank you!"

⊱┈┈⊙┈┈⊰

Kour'el and Api'Naga could not make it all the way to the tower without resting. The man they carried was beginning to awaken and they took advantage of the first thicket of trees to land. It would be better if he wakened on the ground. Kour'el was not sure she could have held him if he had begun to struggle on Api'Naga's back.

They backed away, watching as he moaned and moved. When he opened his eyes his attention focused only on a small pool nearby. Weakly, dragging his chains, he crawled toward it, plunged his face in the water and drank greedily, only stopping when he began to choke and retch.

Soon, thought Kour'el, they would have to try to communicate with him. It would be easier with Api'Naga there. The Great Ones had been able to send thoughts to the humans in her own country just as they did with her own people. Surely he could do the same here.

The man looked up at them and began to shake with fear. Then he slowly backed away until he was hidden beneath some bushes beside the pool. Kour'el felt a surge of pity. At the best of times the poor wretch would be nearly delirious from his ordeal on the city wall. Perhaps he had never seen a dragon before. He had been terrified at the sight of her when she'd first flown to free him — how much more frightening would the sight of even a small Api'Naga be to him? She almost hoped he would become unconscious again. The flight would be easier and they would not have to waste time convincing him to go on with them. They must complete the trip while it was still dark.

We come as friends, Api'Naga was sending. **We wish to help you.**

Kour'el could read no thoughts in the man, only dread

at the sight of the dragon.

Go to him Kour'el. Api'Naga commanded. **Show him that we wish no harm. It is better if I stay back.** And he edged away once more.

Kour'el moved forward, putting herself halfway between the man and the dragon. She wished she could communicate thoughts to reassure him. Instead she sat down, her wings folded flat against her back, and tried to look like one of his own people. She would have to speak, she knew but she was aware of how strange her voice sounded compared to what he was used to. Even though she could imitate their words, the laughing notes, the cadence of her speaking was so different.

"Do not be afraid," she said. She tried again. "Fear not. We come to help you."

The man remained where he was crouched in the bushes but to her relief did not attempt to crawl further into them. Now his thoughts were beginning to have some coherence. He was remembering that it was she who freed him from his awful bondage on the city wall. He was studying her closely now: the pale, almost translucent skin, the shimmering iridescence of her blue-black hair, the delicate limbs, the fluttering white gauzy material that swathed her body. Nothing threatening about her except that she was outside his ken. He was calmer now. She spoke quickly before he could look back at Api'Naga and become alarmed once more.

"Please. We wish you no harm. We want to help you." She could see that he was responding to this reassurance and pressed on. "Why was the queen punishing you?" Perhaps if she gave him something else to concentrate on he would relax and forget that he was speaking to a flying girl and sitting across from a dragon. Even if he did not speak, his thoughts would be useful.

But he did speak. It was the first time she had heard his voice. It was deeper than the men she'd traveled with, but gruff too, unlike the city voices she'd heard in the market. And it was strong now — anger covering his fear.

"I was carrying a message from the king," he said. "A treasonous task these days."

Kour'el waited. He might say more and if he did not, she could learn from his thoughts. At first the emotions covered everything — the anger was too strong — then sorrow.

Ask him where he was going, Api'Naga sent. **Perhaps he will be more apt to tell us that rather than the message itself.**

Clever, thought Kour'el, he might then think of the message and we will learn it that way. She smiled at the man. He seemed more at ease now, had even moved out from beneath the bush.

"Where were you going?" Either her voice was sounding less strange or she was getting used to hearing herself. "Perhaps we can take you there...if you do not mind riding on the dragon's back."

The man looked startled, then a calculating look spread across his features. His thoughts matched his face. Like the old man she'd ridden with, he suspected her of somehow being part of the queen's plotting. He was thinking that what people said about the queen was true — that her charms enslaved the king and that she was able to conjure up legendary creatures to do her bidding.

Kour'el was relieved that she had followed Api'Naga's advice. Had she asked for the message directly it would surely have convinced the man that they were agents of the Queen.

Api'Naga had the same understanding and was quick with a message meant to reassure.

Yes. We could help you go to your destination but we must do so quickly, before daylight. In the day we must hide. The queen's men search for us. We have escaped before but now that we have been seen in the city the search will be even more determined.

Again the man's response was shock he was being spoken to by a dragon — Kour'el realized that he was not aware that it was not speech at all but thoughts. Even so the messenger was not going to betray his destination. She could read the caution in his mind, although Api'Naga's message had caused him to be less suspicious of them.

We can leave you here, Api'Naga tried again, **or we can take you with us**.

"Where are you going?" Mistrust dominated the man's mind.

"We are flying west," Kour'el told him. She was growing more used to speech and she found that if she spoke slowly, her voice was more like people talking. "There is a great forest there near to where I was imprisoned. We hope the queen's soldiers will think we are closer to the city."

This time the man's thoughts showed relief. His destination was also near their forest, a message for someone near there. A name. A title: the King's Hunter.

We must leave soon. Carrying you will slow us.

Kour'el was surprised that Api'Naga was so abrupt. The man might still choose to chance traveling the roads as an ordinary person. He had some lead over his pursuers and was not that weak from only one day without food. She could tell the man was weighing his chances. Best make it all clear to him.

"You will have to sit on..." she hesitated. It was hard for her to refer to Api'Naga merely as dragon, but that was the word in the man's thoughts and it was what he would understand. She hoped the Great One would understand and forgive her disrespect. "...on the dragon's back again."

Don't fret Kour'el. Api'Naga's message to her was amused. **You must make him understand however you can.**

The man was staring at her. He had not been aware of coming here, only of Kour'el freeing him. He had assumed she had carried him. This would be a test of his courage and devotion to the king's cause.

He rose, stumbling a little, surprised at his own weakness but that was enough to convince him that his only chance to avoid capture and deliver his message would be to go with them. Kour'el could not help but admire him as he began to walk toward her and the dragon. The king had chosen well when he'd trusted this man, she decided. She led him toward Api'Naga and was relieved to see him gather his chains and seat himself astride the scaly back. She could sense that he was trembling but was brave enough to hide it.

Quickly, before he could have second thoughts, she lifted and flew above the trees. The countryside was still and dark.

"It is clear," she reported back to Api'Naga and with that the Great One lifted, heavily, for the man was not a small one.

They landed in the forest below the tower. Api'Naga killed another of the hopping creatures and flamed it with his breath, burning off the hairs and leaving the skin crispy and delicious, a hearty meal for the three of them.

She was glad to see that the man they'd rescued no longer seemed fearful. His amazement at watching the Great One cook had amused her so much her laughter had rippled through the forest around them. The man had joined her laughing too until Api'Naga had told them to be more cautious.

We should sleep now, he advised kindly, **in the morning we will try to remove those chains without burning you and you can go on your way to deliver your message.**

Kour'el too gave in to her exhaustion and slept.

CHAPTER SIX

That night was the worst Maighdlin had ever spent. Worry about whether or not she had done the right thing kept her from noticing the pangs of hunger. When at last she drifted off to sleep, her dreams were filled with nightmares of Talun's capture and torture because of her note. She would awaken gasping with fear and lie on the pallet trembling and perspiring. Once she'd even cried out and woken to find the guard standing over her. For a moment that blended into the dream — Talun had confessed and they were coming to take her. After that she had been unable to sleep at all. She had never been so grateful for the glimmer of dawn that told her the night was over.

But the day was not much better. There was no sign of Talun when they lined up to get their breakfast bread. Mala tore hers into chunks and crammed them into her mouth greedily, but Maighdlin could taste nothing though she chewed methodically because she knew she would need her strength.

"You! Come with me!" It was the woman who assigned their daily tasks.

Maighdlin's heart sank. She'd hoped that she and Mala would be working together somewhere out of the way or that she would at last be allowed to go to work in the spinning room. She was sure that she wasn't capable of concentrating: she was sure that her guilt and fear showed on her face and someone would suspect. But there was nothing to do but follow the woman.

She cast a backward glance at Mala. She had not been able to tell her friend about the time in the king's chambers nor about what she had written in the note she'd given Talun. She had signed it by GranDa's name for her, Galea — so that he would know it was truly she who had written it.

She half-expected to be taken to the queen and questioned as in her dreams, but instead to her surprise they seemed to be returning to the king's chamber.

"You are to finish the work you were doing yesterday."

Maighdlin's surprise increased. Servants did not go back to the king's quarters. One of the rules she had been told when she'd arrived was that the king was not to see the same person twice. She'd thought it strange then but she had been here long enough now to know that it was because the queen did not want any servant to befriend him.

When she arrived there the room was empty. The king's bed had been neatly made and the few cushions were stacked nearby.

"The Princess Lurin has commanded that you finish that." The woman pointed to the basket of floss Maighdlin had left undone the day before. "Find yourself a place and stay out of everyone's way!" The woman left nervously as if obeying her own order.

Maighdlin stood alone, taking deep breaths, trying to calm herself. The terror and nightmares of the night before were getting to her. She needed air. Her heart seemed to be trying to pound its way out of her chest. The sound of it filled her ears and she was having trouble breathing. It was as if the room was suffocating her.

The long low window seemed to beckon her. Outside were fresh air and sunshine — the mere thought of it helped. She snatched up the basket and staggered to the window, surprised that her jelly-legs would carry her at all. It was a relief to throw herself across the windowledge — she breathed in the fresh breeze, gasping as if she'd been holding her breath ever since she'd arrived here.

She leaned there, eyes closed, feeling the sunshine on her face. It was only when she began to relax a little that she focused on what was outside. Then she almost laughed out loud. The window was not just a window high above the ground outside, it opened onto a balcony that stretched around the front of the palace. She could be outside on this beautiful day. What better "place to stay out of everyone's way" could there be? Smiling she dropped the basket over the edge and hitched up her skirt to climb over the ledge and slide down the rough stones to the balcony below.

It was perfect there. Beautiful too. Above her the huge amethyst crystals decorating the palace wall caught the light. Rainbows danced all around her. But it was the sunshine and the feel of the soft breeze caressing her face that pleased her most as she began working. She lost herself in the feel of the thread winding against her fingers as she untangled more and more. It was almost as if she was sitting outside her mother's cottage, winding yarn she had spun. It was so familiar and pleasant she could almost forget where she was and what she was doing there; and, for a little while, forget to worry about the young man whose life she had endangered.

She worked well for some time, until the repetition of her movements began to lull her and she drooped onto the brightly colored thread, exhausted from the night's wake-fulness. I will just shut my eyes for a moment, she thought — and slept.

Not far away Petaurus had also spent a long unpleasant night. Luckily no one had entered his hidden stairwell to retrieve fleeces, and the soft wool made a reasonably comfortable bed. But his mind was too full of plans. He could not stay here long. Even though he had brought a bit of food and always carried a flask of water, this was not a safe place to be.

Once the torches were extinguished in the windowless room below, the stairwell hiding place had become pitch dark and he dared not move either up or down on the stairs lest he misstep and break his brittle old bones. He had formed a plan though before he finally slept.

When the torches were lit again in the room below and the people were working there he would try the door at the head of the stairs. If he remembered correctly there was a handle to pull towards you. He would not open it completely, lest he draw attention in the room above. If he waited until night again though he could enter the King's chamber while everyone slept. If it still was the king's chamber.

With light he changed his plan. He tried to rise and climb the stairs but seemed too stiff to do it. What if he made noise? He remembered that the room below had been deserted when he'd entered. Perhaps that happened every day. He would wait. And then if he could not open the door he would try to get to the king in daylight while there was no one about.

He knew he could not spend another night there.

The room where the king now lay was dim and small and although he knew the queen would not dare kill him outright, he feared that the time had come when she would allow him to die. Without help he could not leave — and there was no help. The guards, if there were guards now, were outside the doors and never saw their prisoner. The door opened only at the queen's command, rolling silently inward at the sound of her voice.

Another of her spells. He had only in recent times begun to suspect how many spells there were — how deep she had sunk in her manipulations although once, years ago, he had tried to stop them. If only he had been able to destroy the tower and meet with the ones he'd sent for. Somehow she had turned the dragon against him and mortally wounded the flying one. She had outwitted him and he knew now he had only himself to blame. Then the terrible injuries and the long weeks of pain and her constant presence. He believed then that he owed her his life — that she had changed and would no longer work against him.

But he had not realized then that she needed him, too. Needed to keep him alive — not because she cared for him but because without the king, even ailing, the kingdom would have fallen apart. Now her control was absolute — all obeyed her or died. He had been isolated and now there were none he could turn to. If there were any still loyal to him they could not be reached. Now she did not need him any longer. He could die.

Rumors had reached him that many thought he was

dead. And at those times, there would be an audience with one or two ministers, or he would be propped up to wave to a crowd from the balcony. But the last such occasion had been so long ago, he couldn't remember it.

"Open!" The door slid noiselessly, magically, open.

He turned in the hope of seeing guards — anyone — behind her in the hallway, but she swept in and the door closed in its eerie quiet way too quickly. Even before she spoke he could sense her fury — it was an-all-too familiar mood lately. Still, he welcomed her presence. It was the only news of the outside that he had now.

"Your messenger has escaped!" She spoke between clenched teeth, for once trying to keep her anger under control. "Or should I say..." he could almost taste the bitterness in her voice, "...he has been rescued!"

He tried to keep from registering relief, surprise — any emotion at all. Her eyes were on him, boring into him, measuring his reaction. He said nothing.

She laughed, harshly and with venom. "But you know nothing about this, do you? Nothing but what I tell you, now that you are cut off..." she waved wildly at the barren chamber, "...from everyone but your loving wife!"

Still he maintained composure though his twisted legs ached and he wanted to move them to ease the pain. His silence seemed only to feed her fury.

"I'll tell you then!" she screeched. "A flying girl and a dragon! Did you know there was a dragon about? Smell it?" She paced the small room, then returned and leaned over him, her voice quiet as a snake now. "I did...last night...out on the balcony of your chamber. Why did you think I had you moved? In my hurry to search, I neglected to question you about your reaction to this."

She removed her cloak and waved the fluttering gossamer in his face. It fell limp and lifeless, clinging to him as if to smother him. For the first time since she'd entered he reacted — involuntarily, raising his hand to his face not to push it away but to caress the softness as if he could revive it and himself and so gain some lost strength.

"I knew you knew of the dragon." She spoke quietly now, her voice oozing persuasion. "The one that you summoned all those years ago?" She watched him closely, waiting.

He tried to hide his surprise. He had thought the dragon had turned against him, betrayed him for some reason when it attacked Petaurus and himself there by the tower. Now he wondered if it been not the dragon but some powerful spell of her own protecting the place and her ever-growing power.

"And now you have summoned 'help' again?" Beneath the sugary tones there was steel — and anger. "I let you get too strong. I forgot that you had power too. But..." she laughed, "...we'll soon remedy that!"

The king closed his eyes. It had taken all his strength to send the message and he was not sure it had been received by the Great Ones so far away. He still could not believe that it had. Their long silence and the disappearance of the two who had come before might be the reason for the arrival of these two. They were here and had known enough to rescue the messenger. If only he were not so tired.

There was no food, nothing but a pitcher of water on a stand. He'd been brought to this place in the night, alone, the queen herself pushing the litter. There'd been wine — was it drugged? He had fallen asleep or lost consciousness shortly after they'd left his own chamber, so that he did not know where he was in the palace.

He lay still. He did not want another confrontation with her. It drained his energy, left him even weaker. But even so he was glad she had come — he had learned he was not alone and it gave him hope.

When he opened his eyes he knew she would be gone. He stretched his arm toward the stand but the pitcher was gone. He was without food *or* water. And no-one knew where he was.

He forced himself to examine her plan. She would let him die, of course. There would be a state funeral, a queen in mourning — she'd always looked lovely in black — and then her power would be absolute. She would play the role of the tragic widow and gain sympathy for the noble way she had cared for her invalid and sometimes drunken husband — he knew the rumors had been spread, and sometimes he *had* drunk more wine than he should have, out of boredom and to escape her unpleasantness.

Once he was dead there would be no one to rally behind. The Great One would be forced to abandon the quest and leave. And the kingdom — the kingdom he'd been entrusted to rule and hold — would sink deeper into darkness and fear. Already the people seemed to have forgotten why he was here. First in their happiness at his benevolent rule, and now in fear of the woman he had foolishly brought to share the throne. What was left? A few old songs no one understood anymore and memories of better days.

He attempted to ease his pain by moving his legs and cursed the weakness that had brought him to this state. Fifty years ago — no, it had been more than that — he had been sent by the Great Ones to replace the dying king. Not to start a new dynasty but to hold and wait.

He did not know how he could hold on but he must try. The Great One had come. He must somehow survive a little longer.

CHAPTER SEVEN

---·•·---

Maighdlin was awakened by angry voices coming through the window above her.

"Where is the king?"

Maighdlin recognized the petulant voice of Princess Lurin. She wondered who the luckless servant or courtier would be. The reply came as a shock. The grating voice of Queen Mariah was unmistakable.

"That is none of your concern, my dear. I did not want to tell you or your sisters until now but..." she paused as if trying to lessen the blow of what she was about to say. "Your father has betrayed me..." She corrected herself. "He has betrayed us."

Did Maighdlin detect a sob in the voice? Hard to believe, but perhaps it was a play for her daughter's sympathy.

"How?" Princess Lurin sounded incredulous. "We watched him every minute."

The voices were fading now. They must be moving out of the room or beyond into another chamber.

"Where is he?" The princess repeated her earlier question..

"It is probably just as well that you don't know. He is in a safe place where no servants or...." The rest of the queen's answer was lost to Maighdlin. They had evidently left.

So, she had risked Talun's life for nothing. She had hoped somehow that she might somehow get GranDa's reply to the king, but a message would be useless if she could not find him. Perhaps it was hopeless.

It was much warmer than when she'd first come out onto the balcony. She wondered how long she had slept. Her mouth was dry and now her thirst made all other concerns seem minor. She must have a drink. There was still much floss to untangle so she left the basket and slipped inside. She was sure there had been a flagon of wine by the king's bedside. Servant gossip was that the queen made a point of keeping the king's wine glass filled so that he was in a drunken state much of the time. Maighdlin wondered at this — she had seen no sign of drunkenness when he'd spoken to her.

Yes, there it was. Water would be better to quench her thirst but she was desperate. The wine tasted heavy and strong but it did moisten her throat.

A sip was all she had time for, suddenly there were voices outside the door — coming closer.

Maighdlin's heart stopped. Without the basket of yarn she had no excuse being here. And she recognized one of the voices: Princess Lurin.

There was no time to return to the window and no hiding place. Getting beneath the king's bed was hopeless — it extended to the floor. The largest thalycine hide nearby was the only thing. It hung from the wall behind the dais. If no one looked carefully — if the princess was absorbed in her anger enough — Maighdlin just might be unnoticed in the folds. There was no time to think. She slipped behind and stood petrified. Too afraid to wonder if below the skin her feet might be showing. All she could do was hold her breath and hope that the dusty old hide didn't provoke a sneeze.

"I sent you for the basket and you say it is not here?" The princess's voice could be almost as shrill as her mother's when she was upset.

Maighdlin's heart fell. If they searched the room, they would surely notice something amiss — the bulge in the skin. She pressed against the wall wishing the stones would open and hide her, and only felt them painfully digging into her back.

"Did you check the next room?" The princess was still irritated but with any luck the servant or guard might escape with only shattered nerves — if the basket were not found.

"Yes, your Highness. " A man's voice — a guard then.

Maighdlin could hear them move into the next room. Was there time to rush to the window? Whatever was poking her in the back was really hurting. She turned and saw it was a lever, its iron deeply rusted. Was there a secret door? Praying that the lever would not creak too loudly — she could hear the voice of the princess returning — Maighdlin pushed it downward.

The door flew open and Maighdlin tumbled head over heels to land at the feet of her grandfather.

Petaurus helped Maighdlin up and then saw they were not alone. A guard stood at the top of the stairs looking down at them.

Behind him an imperious female voice. "What's going on? Is there someone hiding there?"

Petaurus held onto his granddaughter. He would die protecting her. He tried to push her behind him but she did not want to be hidden. And the guard was behaving strangely. He stepped back and let the flap hiding the door fall. Petaurus knew he had seen them clearly but the words he heard were not what he expected.

"There is no one there, your Highness."

Maighdlin was tugging him now, pulling him to go on down the steps out of sight. But the doorway was uncovered too quickly. The princess stood glaring down at them.

"Seize them!" When the guard did not move quickly enough she turned back to him. "Don't you hear me, dolt? Why don't you act?" She was moving back through the doorway. "I'll get more guards. You keep them here... if you are capable of anything, fool!"

But the doorway was blocked and instead of obeying her commands and rushing to arrest the two below, the young man seized the princess and clamped his hand over her mouth.

Maighdlin was horrified. "Talun!"

And then to Petaurus' dismay he heard voices in the room below become louder. The workers had noticed a disturbance in the stairwell, and were coming to see what it was. As quickly and quietly as he could he began to climb the stairs behind Maighdlin. The door closed silently behind him as they entered the room he remembered so well: the king's chamber.

"Where is the king?" He turned to the princess, demanding again, "Where is he?"

Talun was about to remove his hand from her mouth but Maighdlin stopped him. "She doesn't know. The queen has moved him somewhere...no one knows."

There was an angry squeal from the princess and she tore at Talun's hands.

"Have you something to say?" Talun asked. Lurin nodded angrily. "Do you swear that you will not scream?" Another angry nod. He removed his hand from Lurin's mouth and directed all his energy to restraining the frenzied young woman. She did not scream. Instead, her eyes dark with fury, she began to take deep breaths. Sucking in the air like a bellows, she seemed to glow in Talun's arms. Then she turned to him and exhaled. Flames!

So that was why they called her Firegirl, Maighdlin thought in shock.

Talun fell away from the flame, releasing Princess Lurin. She was breathing deeply again and Maighdlin did not wait to see how long it would take for another blast. She seized the silver flask that held the wine. Talun and Petaurus might be reluctant to hit a woman, especially a princess, but she was not. Wine splashed everywhere as the heavy flask connected with a satisfying thud, and Lurin fell to the floor.

The three of them stood in stunned silence. Talun's face was reddened as if with a deep sunburn but he had been able to extinguish his jacket sleeve so that it was only singed a little.

Petaurus spoke first. "I think we will have to take her with us. She may not be missed for yet awhile and we will be able to make our escape."

Talun bent and picked her up. "There are no guards, only a few maids doing the cleaning in this part of the royal quarters...after that though...." He shook his head hopelessly.

"I know of a passage out of the royal chambers." Maighdlin rushed ahead, checking outside the door to make sure the corridors were really clear. "Follow me!"

She went first, casually checking at each open door to

be sure there was no one to see them pass. She was hoping against hope that the room she wanted would be empty but as she neared the doorway she could hear a voice. She waved the others to wait as she looked in the room. Were there two within? No, there appeared to be just one maid, partly hidden by the tapestries. One maid grumbling to herself. Mala! Almost laughing with relief she turned and beckoned Petaurus and Talun to enter, then quickly closed the door.

Mala emerged, hair mussed and dusty from her work.

"What's.... Maighdlin, what's going on? Petaurus, how did...?" She moved closer. "Great Gremlins! What have you done with the princess?" She sounded shocked but not unhappy about Lurin's fate.

"Thank goodness it's you, Mala!" Maighdlin's relief showed in her voice. Now if they succeeded in escaping she needn't worry about any repercussions to her friend. And even better, Mala could take the torches and lead the way down the passage. Maighdlin yawned. She was beginning to feel unbelievably sleepy.

The passageway sloped sharply, winding deeper and deeper into the bowels of the palace. Though it was easier than climbing, Maighdlin got more tired with every step. Why was she so drowsy? Surely one sip of wine could not have this effect.

Finally she could bear it no longer. "I have to sit a minute," she said and sank to the stone floor. "Go on, I'll catch up." The others were already ahead. Even Talun with his load of unconscious princess was making better time.

The others clustered around her urging her on. "Nonsense, Maighdlin," said GranDa firmly. "We can't possibly leave you."

"What's wrong?" There was concern in Talun's voice. "Are you ill?"

Maighdlin shook her head wearily. "No. I drank...some of the king's wine...just a sip...but it made me sleepy."

Petaurus looked grim. "Probably drugged." He bent to lift her but did not have the strength.

"We'll just have to dump the princess in this alcove so Talun can carry you." Mala had moved ahead and was pointing to a small closet-like room off the tunnel. She did not look too sorry at the idea of abandoning Lurin. "Nobody comes this way except that old serving woman, and now that I think of it I haven't seen her for a few days.... maybe the queen's got rid of her." Her voice was bitter, "...the way she did Salena."

Maighdlin allowed them to lift her and for a while she stumbled along, propped up and propelled by Mala. Luckily the stairs had ended and the way was flat. The damp stones under foot showed they must be well underground though the torch flickered eerily so there must be air entering above them.

"Strange. I never heard the king speak of this passage." GranDa mused. "We must be leaving the palace, perhaps even going beyond the city." The passageway was straight now stretching on into darkness beyond the flickering torchlight.

At last Maighdlin gave up. Even with Mala's help she could walk no more. She slumped to the ground and slept.

Chapter Eight

Kour'el did not waken until late the next day. The shadows had already begun to deepen. She had been so exhausted yesterday — she must have been sleeping very soundly. The man was gone. His chains lay in a heap. She had not even heard Api'Naga remove them.

Api'Naga lay nearby. He looked to be resting though with the Great Ones it was hard to tell. They often achieved a deep meditative state that was easily confused with sleep or even death. She watched him carefully, relieved to see the gentle movement of his scaled side that indicated he was breathing.

She was glad to be the only one awake. This would give her time to think. Something yesterday puzzled her. She had missed something and she knew it was important. Her illness had taught her a great deal about connecting the pieces of a puzzle.

During the trip her concern had been rescuing the man, getting away, then getting him to trust them. He had trusted them enough to come along but not enough to reveal the message the king had given him, not even in his thoughts.

But she had read something in his thoughts. A name. The King's Hunter. Petaurus....

She moved excitedly, lifting a few feet off the ground in the thrill of her discovery. It was the name of the old man in the cart! The man who wanted to see the king, who was going to the palace to rescue his granddaughter. The man who had thought Kour'el was a spy for the queen. The man carrying the piece of her wing!

That is useful information, Kour'el! Api'Naga had either not been sleeping or had been wakened by her movement. **So our messenger will not be able to deliver his message...if his quarry is still in the city. I wonder if he will come back to us.**

Kour'el wondered too. — Shall I fly up and see if I can see him? She was sure she could skim the tree tops and dip down in clearings, remaining unnoticed provided she did not leave the forest. But it was not necessary. They could hear the man approaching and soon he was back with them.

All trace of yesterday's fear and suspicion had gone. He threw himself down beside the two of them. "I have failed," he said, "my man is gone...to the city." The man looked tired and pale from his morning's exertion. Walking through the forest to the village and back had drained his strength. And he was still in obvious pain from the burns though someone in the village had treated and bandaged his wrists expertly.

Kour'el let Api'Naga explain that she had remembered about Petaurus. It was easier for him to send the thoughts than for her to tell such a long story in difficult speech.

There was no doubt that the man now trusted them completely for he looked relieved as he spoke.

"Then my task has really been accomplished...for my message was to tell Petaurus that the king wished to see him." He looked at Kour'el thoughtfully. "Still, it would be good if the King's Hunter could be told. It would make it easier for him...if someone could fly the message to him in the city."

Kour'el was delighted at an excuse to fly again. It would be dark soon and she sensed Api'Naga's approval.

You may go alone...it is easier for you to travel unnoticed. I will remain behind. Carrying our friend here was more exhausting than I would have thought possible and I could use a chance to build up my strength.

It was a good plan and Kour'el felt a thrill of pride that he trusted her to go. It was not until she was flying, joying in the freedom and tasting the sweet night air, that it occurred to her to wonder what she would do if the old man still mistrusted her. But it was not in her nature to dwell on negative thoughts. Her kind lived in the moment, always looking for the best and although she had changed in her imprisonment she still had that ability. She would have to convince Petaurus that was all.

She hoped that she would find them somewhere outside the city not far from where they had picked her up. But there was no sign of them. No sign of any of the people who left the city each night. Were people no longer allowed to come and go? There was nothing for it but to go look for him in the marketplace.

She considered trying to find a cloak and walking into the square but that would take time and she knew that the guards would question anyone roaming the streets at night. She decided to hover above the walls and look for the donkeys and cart and risk the danger of someone looking up.

She had no trouble spotting the cart. It was where they had parked it the day she'd ridden with them. Yes, there was the young man. She could not see the older one but perhaps he was lying out of sight asleep.

She swooped down, landing silently beside the young man. Almost instantly she could hear shouts from the guards on the wall. She did not have much time.

Luckily the young man was awake. She read worry and then as he saw her — alarm.

"Petaurus?" she said, trying to make her voice sound the way he would expect it. He did not answer but his thoughts made her heart sink. The older man had gone to the palace the day before yesterday and had not returned. She could tell the young man was worried, almost frantic with the strain of waiting and not knowing what had happened.

She had been lucky. There had been no guards in the immediate area but now there were shouts and running feet. She could leave now but she would have accomplished nothing.

"Let me carry you over the wall, so we can talk." She started lifting and tried to get hold of him from behind under the arms, as she had the prisoner, but he drew back fearfully. There was no time to argue. She said the one word she knew might convince him. "Marika!"

It worked. She seized him and flew straight up until she was out of arrow range, then glided over the palace walls. If Marika was in the palace then it must appear that was where they were going so that he would be at ease. Luckily, he was lithe and lean and weighed less than the prisoner she had carried before, so he was not nearly so difficult. She flew to one of the only two places she knew of in the palace, the dragon courtyard.

In the darkness the statues loomed eerily. She had not given any thought to what the young man's reaction would be to the strange beasts — she had only wanted some place where they might talk undisturbed.

"Marika!" He demanded without even looking around him. "What do you know of Marika?"

Kour'el realized that it would take some time for his eyes to adjust to the darkness. There was a dim light coming from a single torch burning in a sconce by the doorway beyond them but it only succeeded in casting weird shadows and was not of much help where they were. She could see well already — her eyes adjusted quickly for flying at night. She had already been able look about to make sure that they were alone. She folded her wings and sat down on one of the stone benches to rest, pretending to be getting her breath back. How could she explain that all she knew of Marika was what she had read in his thoughts that day they had traveled together?

Before she could stop him, the young man ran swiftly to the torch, seized it and brought it back to where they were. He looked at her now, the light flickering in her face. She read recognition in his thoughts. He was remembering the almost transparent skin, the iridescent hair sparkling in the torchlight. It was unbound now and rippled about her head almost as if it had a life of its own, the way it always did when she had flown.

After a moment he moved the torch away from her face. "It is you, isn't it? You are the girl on the road that day. I thought you had something terribly wrong with your back but they were your...your *wings*.." He laughed ruefully. "And I felt so sorry for you!" He was excited now. "Are you the flying one that freed the queen's prisoner?"

Kour'el nodded. She began to be caught up in his excitement. He had the same bursts of enthusiasm and joy that her people did. She like his impetuousness and she understood him perfectly as his thoughts shifted quickly to something that puzzled him.

"Petaurus wouldn't talk about you but I could tell he was upset."

It was time for her to risk speaking. She chose her words and spoke slowly — as clearly as she could.

"Petaurus thought I was a spy for the queen."

The practice she'd had talking to the prisoner had been good. She was able to control her voice better, keep it from trilling away giving the words the wrong emphasis. She waited to make sure that he understood and then continued. "I am *not* a spy...the queen is my enemy too."

She would let him absorb that information before she went on to tell him about the messenger and why she sought the old man he'd traveled with. She wanted to learn all she could of Petaurus — and put off the moment Brede learned that she did not intend to take him to Marika at all.

>─┼─◦──◦─┼─◦

Marika could not sleep. That day she'd received a message from Brede: Petaurus had gone to the palace and not returned. Thanks to the palace grapevine Marika was sure no trespasser had been arrested — that was always big news. Marika marveled at how much she had learned since she first arrived. The servants managed to note and discuss even the disappearance or deaths of people in the secretive royal apartments. The identities of grapevine key connections were never mentioned but it was a comfort to know that there was this unity among the servants, and people who had not given up. And these had shared the news that an older man from the country had been seen entering the palace the day after the execution of the last group of "rebels".

Marika tossed and turned. She wondered how Maighdlin was. She racked her brain for a possible explanation of why no one had seen Petaurus. There were servants who would help him, if he were lucky enough to find one — even a few guards who were sympathetic enough to carry messages. She had received one from Maighdlin herself, from the guard who'd accompanied them from Blue Mountain village, and Marika had sent on Maighdlin's note for Petaurus this way.

Had he received it? Or had it gone to Brede? She worried about Brede. How long would he be able to put up with doing nothing, waiting alone in the marketplace?

She sat up. She was too restless to sleep. She had to get up. Perhaps if she went to relieve herself — she would say it was an emergency. But both guards were sound asleep. This wasn't unusual. One of the new girls had once sleep-walked right by the sleeping guards, and was found wandering in a corridor some distance away.

Marika did not have a plan but once outside she found she wanted only one thing — a window. She had been cooped up in the lower part of the palace for so long. She yearned to feel the night air on her face. She told herself that if she were discovered she could feign sleep-walking.

She tried several corridors lookiing for stairs. At last she found some steps and began to climb. At the top she found herself in a corridor that seemed to wind around the upper part of the palace. She came to a window and leaned out, drinking in the fresh night air. She would stay here until the terrible suffocating feeling went away, and then slip quietly back the way she had come. Then she opened her eyes, and discovered she could see.

Below her lay the sleeping city and beyond the city walls the darkened countryside. Though she could not see the Blue Mountain beyond, she imagined the sleeping village and her mother's cottage with its fragrant herb bundles hanging everywhere. The comfort that she had gained from the fresh air vanished and she began to weep silently. She had never felt so alone.

Slowly she regained her composure and with it came fear at her own foolishness for coming here. What was she doing? She had to be sensible. It served no purpose to risk her life. Perhaps by now Petaurus would have returned to the marketplace. Tomorrow she would surely hear something. She must be patient and not take risks. She had been lucky not to have been seen on the way here. Perhaps her luck would hold and she could make it back safely.

She was trembling now more from fear than from the chill of the night air. She slipped along the corridor and had just begun to descend the stone steps when she heard heavy footsteps further down the stairs below. Without thinking, Marika turned and fled back the way she had come. Now she raced silently past the windows, the view of the sleeping city only a blur out of the corner of her eye. In vain she searched for an alcove, a doorway to hide behind but there was nothing. She could no longer hear the footsteps and there had been no voices so perhaps there was only one guard — it would surely be a guard at this hour. Someone who was supposed to be there patrolling the corridors and had no need to muffle his footsteps.

She rounded the bend into deepening darkness. She had to stop her headlong flight. Now she even regretted it.

Why hadn't she just stayed where she was and used her sleepwalking excuse? The further away from her quarters she was when discovered, the less likely it was she would be believed.

She tried to listen for footsteps but all sound seemed to be drowned out by her panting and the pounding of her heart, the rush of blood in her ears. The guard had to come this way. There were no options once on the stairs — unless he turned and went back.

Of course! That was what guards on patrol did — they walked a certain distance and then turned and went back. Perhaps he only walked to the head of the stairs and then returned. She was safe.

Gradually she calmed. She moved across to look out a window she had not even noticed before. She would get her breath and start back. It was all she could think to do.

She did not make it to the window. She sensed that there was someone in the darkness before she heard him and by that time he had seized her arm.

Forgetting all pretense of sleepwalking Marika struggled to free herself from the man's grip. It was a silent struggle. Although he had surprised her she did not allow more than a gasp before she gritted her teeth and began to fight.

The guard had not cried out either though they were supposed to sound the alarm when they found anyone trespassing near the royal quarters. But this girl would be no challenge, and besides, he could see she was young and lovely. The queen would not care what condition she was in when he dragged his prisoner to her Majesty later on. Still, he had not expected such a wildcat.

Marika was strong. She had often play-wrestled with

Brede when they were children and he had taught her some fighting technique though she knew he always let her win and was careful not to hurt her.

The only sound in the silent struggle was the clang of the guard's helmet on the stones when Marika knocked it off.

The sound of the helmet falling rang like a bell in the courtyard below. Kour'el's sharp ears caught the muffled noise of the struggle. Brede's hearing was acute too and both looked up with the same thought.

"Petaurus! Perhaps he has been discovered and captured," Brede said beneath his breath.

It was worth investigating. Without a word Kour'el lifted to the windows above the courtyard where she'd heard the noise.

The girl was definitely losing the struggle. Kour'el saw that if the guard would let go of his victim she could just sweep her up and fly out again. But he was holding her too tightly. Kour'el's people were not fighters, but she realized that she would have to help this girl escape somehow. She wished she'd brought the young man but she was on her own. Perhaps she could startle the guard into letting go. She lifted and softly began the flight song. It worked. The man dropped the girl and turned his attention to Kour'el.

She had not noticed the knife at his belt until he drew it and came toward her. He would be easy to evade she realized and she could get by him to the girl quite easily. But now she realized the flaw in her plan. He would immediately sound the alarm and she would have two people to remove from the palace, and no time to do it.

The girl solved the problem. She picked herself up and

there was a second clang. This time it was the helmet connecting with the guard's head hard enough to stun him.

Kour'el had no time to explain herself. She did not even have time to look closely at the girl she had rescued until she set her down beside the young man in the courtyard below. Then Brede and Kour'el, reading his recognition, looked at the shocked girl standing before them and spoke in unison. "Marika!"

Kour'el left them together. She could not have pried them apart anyway. She flew quickly back to the guard — she had to get him away before he regained consciousness and sounded the alarm. He was heavy and she knew she could not fly far with him, but the palace had some interesting turrets surrounding the courtyard on the other side. They were high enough that he would find it difficult to get down easily. She hoped that would give her time to get her two young lovers away.

But when the guard came to and began to struggle, it was too much for Kour'el. She dropped him with a thud into the dark courtyard she was flying over. She followed and found him lying peacefully in the roses. It would take some time for him to explain how he'd got there when he came to next.

Streaks of light were beginning to show in the eastern sky and Kour'el knew the dragon would wonder why she had not returned. Soon it would not be safe to fly. It was slow going, carrying the maiden, she would have to return for the young man.

She was halfway to the forest when she heard Api'Naga's sending.

Kour'el! Kour'el! If anyone sleeping or waking below sensed the message it would mean nothing to them. A

strange ringing in their head, a haunting double note —
nothing more.

A moment later Api'Naga swooped down to meet her.
Marika thought they were being attacked and clung to
Kour'el, making flying difficult, and Api'Naga quickly flew
away again, waiting above until Kour'el had returned to
the palace courtyard and sent to him to come.

Kour'el hastily tried to still their fear. It bothered her
that the people in this land feared the Great Ones. They
were the most benevolent and kindly of all creatures. She
would not have believed any would fear them. It was different in her own land. But here they even feared a harmless flying creature like herself.

As he had with the messenger Api'Naga patiently
remained at a distance until Kour'el had reassured them.
Then she explained that if Brede would ride on the dragon's
back they might still get to their destination before the sun
rose.

— They are from the village near the forest, she sent to
Api'Naga. And the man Petaurus has disappeared.

CHAPTER NINE

The king was dying.

Sometimes in moments of lucidity he wondered how he had come to this so quickly. He was sure he had only been without food and water for only a day or, at most, two. Had the wine been drugged with more than just a sleeping draft? A slow-acting poison might be causing this.

The queen had not returned. He was sure she would come once again before he died, if only to gloat over him or try to make him beg forgiveness once again. If she had managed to torture his message from the servant, she would know now that he had been sending to Petaurus to tell him the time had come for the long-ago plan to be fulfilled and for help to escape from her.

He turned to face the wall. The mattress he lay upon was covered with rough homespun that chafed his cheeks above his beard. He choked at the smell of it. The only advantage to having no food or water was that he was not in a worse state.

When he had last been conscious the room had been dark. Now it must be morning for the sun streamed in from somewhere above him lighting the strange scratching on the wall beyond. Arcane symbols for some spell of hers, no doubt. He would not even try to see what they were. But the window gave him some hope. Perhaps he could pull himself up. He had been a tall man and if he could only reach the ledge he might look out and understand where he was. Not that it would help. There were many turrets and hidden rooms in the palace that no one ever went near.

Slowly he dragged himself into the middle of the room, the stones scraping painfully against his tender flesh — invalid flesh. The window was not barred as he had expected. That was strange. Even stranger, it looked as if there had been bars but they were gone, not broken but left as lumpen metal.

But there was nothing to grasp on the stone wall and there was no strength in his legs to raise himself. There was nothing he could do. He fought against the hopelessness. There must be something. What had she said when she came? Another Great One had come. Not alone for she'd worn the wings of one of the bird people who served them. So she had destroyed them again. Or had she? She claimed that he had called them. But he could not believe that — he was too weak.

'Until you recognize your true enemy, you cannot fight — until you fight, you cannot win', it said in the ancient writings. For too long he had refused to accept how truly evil she was. Always he had blamed himself, blamed others, and he had to admit, he'd been dazzled by her beauty and her constant attention. Why would someone so striking, so exquisite, be bothered with a man wasted by illness as he was? He had been grateful for so long, realizing too late that it was not good fortune but a great curse.

He lay there, too weak and weary to drag himself back to the foul-smelling pallet. Here at least he could see the sky. At least he would have that as he died. Storm clouds had covered the sun now. He could smell that distinctive, almost electric odor that came just before the rain. Strange how a familiar smell could bring comfort. Like the smell of the Great One in the courtyard that night. It was painful to think there had been help so close at hand. She accused him of sending for them but he had not done so, could not have sent so far from within the shielding of the palace walls. But if they were here why not try? It might take what little strength he had left but it would be worth it.

The king raised his head, stared through the window above him and concentrated all his remaining energy on the thought, focusing it on the clouds above him. For moments he stayed as if frozen and then collapsed on the stones and was still.

>–+–◆❯–•–❮◆+–❮

Kour'el woke from an exhausted sleep, her arms aching from the exertions of the night before. The last of the traveling had been done in the dawn light. Flying close to the deserted tower and down to the forest they avoided Blue Mountain village in the hope that no one would see them. Api'Naga stayed awake to guard. Now as the sun streamed through the thick branches above, the Great One slept. So did the young couple they'd brought with them. But the messenger — Geraint was the name he gave — was awake, sitting staring into a tiny smokeless fire he had kindled to take away the early morning chill. Kour'el moved toward it. She longed to feel the glow that always began inside and then brought a tingling warmth as she floated and drifted skyward caressed by the morning sun with its fresh scents and its cascading birdsong. She sighed and held out her hands to the fire — it was a poor way to get warm but safe, at least.

The man nodded toward Api'Naga who stirred in his sleep. "Your friend has been very restless. Do dragons have bad dreams?" He smiled as if pleased with his joke.

Kour'el was pleased at it too. It meant that the man was no longer afraid, that he had accepted them as friends. She turned to look at the place where the Great One slumbered and noticed for the first time that the forest floor about him was disturbed by his movements. That *was* unusual. As she watched he stirred again, his wings twitching, his body tossing from side to side. He flung his head in the air but did not awaken.

— Api'Naga, she sent as she moved toward him. What is wrong? She knelt now, touching his head, pulling away when he shook her off. But she was relieved to see that his eyes opened and now he rose with his usual dignity to face her.

I dreamed, he sent and Kour'el could sense his embarrassment. Dreams and nightmares were the stuff of humans and bird people. She had never heard of such a thing among the Great Ones — they did not dream — they *knew*.

We were on a quest and we had failed. There was a call for help but it was so weak...too weak.... He looked around helplessly.

This too was unlike Api'Naga. This confusion. It saddened her. She had to try to cheer him up. — Could it have been real? Not a dream... she sent. Someone sending the old way? Someone here?

He turned to her hopefully.

— Listen now...perhaps it will come again.

They sat quietly, waiting. At last she felt his disappointment in the sending, **Nothing. It is as if there was nothing but emptiness. And yet...I would like it to have been real.**

Kour'el stood. — Then I think we should treat it as though it were. Someone too weak to waken you. Did you have a sense of its direction?

Api'Naga turned and faced away from her. **This way...I think. No, I am sure. When it is night we can fly in that direction and search.**

— Perhaps we shouldn't wait for night. Perhaps we should walk toward it. As long as we do not fly we should be safe. We would hear someone coming in the forest.

And, she told herself, if it is real and it comes again we will be ready.

You are right...if it is real. He had read her private thoughts again.

Kour'el turned and began to explain to Geraint that they were going. She was pleased that her speech was almost like a human's now.

The man waited. "Let me come. These two do not need protection, do they?" He nodded toward the sleeping couple, "...after all they are close to home. But if you meet anyone hunting in the forest, you can hide and I can speak to them and perhaps learn something. We still do not know what became of the man I was sent to find."

Api'Naga answered before Kour'el could. **They will be safe,** he agreed. **Let him come.**

The three set out moving silently through the forest, Geraint leading. The sun was high above as they reached the path Kour'el remembered climbing the day she'd been captured. She could see the stones of the wall above them. She glanced at Api'Naga and realized that he too recognized it. Around the curve of the cliff was the barren hillside where his last battle had taken place, where dragon blood had wiped out all life it had touched and where nothing would grow again.

Neither sent a specific thought but each wrapped the other in sympathy.

The man was not aware and paused at the base of the path. "Do you want to go on...? Is there a way beyond the wall?"

"Shall we?" Kour'el sent to Api'Naga. "There is an opening in the wall if I could find it again...and beyond that, the tower where..." She shuddered and knew that the Great One understood.

We will be exposed with no hope of hiding should anyone come this way but if worse comes to worst we can always fly.

He seemed to be less doubtful now, Kour'el thought. No longer troubled by doubts of the message — and this must be the way.

It is...I am, he sent.

It was all Kour'el needed, she would follow and do what she could. It was Api'Naga's quest now.

Kour'el's first sight of the tower after they had slipped through the wall was not what she had expected. What had she expected? Fear? The memory of her painful recovery? She was not sure. It looked innocent from this distance bathed in sunshine, like some ancient ruin. Even though it triggered memories of her fall and of the queen and the soldiers there was none of the terror that had filled her dreams when she'd been prisoner.

It seemed so long ago that this had first begun, when she'd first stood in that darkened place and listened to the voice of the Great One who'd sent her. Why had she been sent with so little information? Someone had disappeared — there had been no word for a long time. She tried to put herself back into that closed darkness so that she could remember every word.

Api'Naga turned to her. At first she thought his intense look meant he had another sending as in the dream, then she realized he had read her thoughts again. **That one who disappeared...who had not sent word for a long time,** he sent, **that could be one of the others...like you and me. The dragon and the flying girl who did not return — perished here** — he looked towards the coppery lake, the barren hillside she had seen from the tower window — **as we almost did. Try to remember. Was there anything else to help us? Any clue as to why *they* came?**

Kour'el shook her head. Nothing. She felt the Great One's support and tried once again to remember the darkness. It seemed so long ago, she'd been so innocent. Her first assignment. Her memories were tangled with her own thoughts at that time: relief that Api'Naga was to be her companion and the niggling feeling that this was a hopeless assignment, that someone inexperienced was being sent because of that. She would not be missed if the cause were lost — not flattering at all. Vainly she tried to weed out her own misgivings and simply remember instructions. But there were so few. She'd dreamed it once but had she missed something? Yes! She remembered now — some reference to a ship. No, that word had not been used — the Great One had referred to a vessel.

A vessel is not always a ship, it can be a cup. It can be a container to hold something.

But there had been something else. Some clue. A name.

That was it! She sensed Api'Naga's relief. She had forgotten that there had been a name.

So there was someone to contact.

Kour'el must not force her memory. She felt it was almost coming to her, a name flickering somewhere just out of reach but if she forced herself it would be gone. She began to skirt around. A name. She could read Api'Naga's impatience — it was uncharacteristic and it jolted her and the elusive memory faded, and with it, the name. Despair swept over her.

Too late Api'Naga tried to calm her. For the second time in all her captivity and searches Kour'el wept.

————•••————

Queen Mariah sat in the dragon courtyard glaring at the most recent statue, the one Kour'el had glimpsed and named "The Death of Api'Naga." Anyone examining it would have been impressed by how amazingly lifelike it was and then on closer examination considered how unfortunate it was that it was broken. The dragon was missing a great piece that appeared to have been sliced from its haunch. A piece that did not seem to have fallen nearby for the ground around it was clear.

Mariah rose and paced angrily back and forth. Where was Lurin? The girl had been hiding since yesterday. She had ordered a guard to find her some time ago and there was still no sign of the princess. The queen would tolerate no disobedience, even in her own daughter. It was a disquieting thought but Mariah had noticed signs of independence in her youngest daughter recently. Perhaps it had been a mistake to have given her some of the dragon's power. She would have kept it herself but she'd chosen to take the power of the wings and she'd been feeling generous — Lurin's admiration for her was flattering. But the dragon's breath had been greatly weakened in the death and transferring.

"Your Majesty." The guard stood at the entrance of the courtyard nearby. The queen had given orders that only members of the royal family could walk here. Her angry acknowledgment caused the young man to take an involuntary step backward.

"Please, Your M-M-Majesty, I cannot l-l-locate her Highness the Princess Lurin."

"Well *search* for her."

The guard was cringing. "Yes, your Majesty, s-s-servants and courtiers are s-s-searching."

Damn the girl! She would be made to wait when she did show up. It would serve Lurin right for being so headstrong and ignoring her.

Mariah waved away the guard in disgust. He backed away so quickly he smashed his head against one of the sconces beside the archway.

There is one person who can't get away from me now, Mariah thought grimly. Perhaps it was time the devoted wife paid one last visit to her ailing husband.

She strode from the courtyard and the expression on her exquisite face boded ill for any servant or courtier who crossed her path.

>-+<>-O-<>-+-<

"Are you sure you don't want me to carry you?" Talun turned to ask Maighdlin.

Mala stifled a giggle as Maighdlin shook her head. It was the third time he had asked that question since Maighdlin had woken from her drugged stupor.

Maighdlin had wakened suddenly. "GranDa! Where is he? I didn't dream that did I?" She began to struggle and Talun set her down. "Mala!" There had been panic in her voice. "You're here! Where's GranDa?" Then she had turned and seen him and struggled upright to throw her arms around him in a joyful hug. Soon she looked happily at the others. "It wasn't a dream...thank you Talun. We're still in the tunnel?" At last she calmed down a little and groaned and put her hand to her forehead, "I've got a raging headache...."

Now it seemed they had been walking for hours. Mala was walking more and more slowly and Petaurus was having problems keeping up. One torch had been used up and the one Mala now carried, flickered fitfully. Soon it would go out and they would be in complete darkness.

"I think we'd better stop," Petaurus said as he sank wearily to the floor. Talun crouched beside them. "We should all rest now anyway — we've come a long way and should be safe here for some time."

Mala sank gratefully to the floor. It was damp and they'd probably all feel stiff before too long but it was such a relief to sit down. The torch was burning dangerously low. Petaurus nodded toward it and spoke.

"We'll be losing light soon. We must prepare for that...I suppose we can link arms and use the wall to guide us."

"The tunnel has got to end somewhere, I suppose." Talun sounded hopeful. "If it did not mean leaving you in darkness, I would try to scout on ahead but..."

Maighdlin looked concerned but Mala ignored him. Let him do whatever he wished, she would get as comfortable as possible and rest. She untied her apron and rolled it into a bundle to use as a pillow. She didn't care if it was dark or light, she was going to try to sleep. Something lumpy against her cheek — she should have emptied the pockets. All the maids' aprons had large pockets to carry the dusting rags. That should have made it softer but — of course, she'd been replacing candles in the chambers she'd dusted and she'd tucked the stubs into her apron to get rid of later. She scrambled up and began to remove them — one, two, three, four — there were five and two were of a good length.

Quickly she lit one of them and handed the torch and the other longest candle to Talun. "Now you can explore while we rest." She lay back on her apron pillow and closed her eyes. The sound of his boots on the stones faded in the distance as she fell asleep.

Then Maighdlin was shaking her shoulder gently. Talun had come back far too soon as far as Mala was concerned. She struggled to get up, amazed to find that her body could ache in so many places. She felt as if she'd been trampled by a mob but she said nothing. If it was this bad for her it would be a thousand times worse for Petaurus but he said nothing, only allowed Maighdlin to help him as he rose stiffly to his feet.

"It is not far now," Talun said, "soon it slants upwards and there is a spiral stairway...and the place above it seems to be deserted."

"It must not be far." Mala noticed that the torch he carried burned brightly. "You didn't even need to use the candles."

"I did use them, for a moment. I was on the stairs when the torch began to die and I lit the candles. Then I found this torch...and lit it and left the burned one."

"If there is a torch ready and waiting then perhaps someone is using the place..." murmured Petaurus. "You heard nothing?"

"No. It seemed deserted. Eerie though...a moaning like the wind..so I expect that there is an opening...a window or something...I did not dare stay too long."

"Talun, " Petaurus said falling into step with the young man, "describe the stairway and everything you saw...if it is where I think it is...and if we can find a way out of it...we'll be home in Blue Mountain before too long."

━┿━◆━○━◆━┿━

The Princess Lurin was aware of nothing at first but the worst headache she'd ever known. It took her mind off the fact that she couldn't move to call that wretched maid. Why was she sleeping like this? Her legs ached from being crunched and her throat was painful — she wanted a drink and a cloth for her throbbing head. Where was that bloody maid?

Gradually she remembered: people hiding off the king's chamber, and that insolent guard who'd disobeyed and then tried to hold her. It cheered her to remember how she'd got him with the dragon's fire. She allowed herself a happy dream of revenge — she'd baste him like a turkey when she got out of here.

Where was she anyway? Crammed like butterfly in a cocoon in some place dark as pitch. She wiggled until she was sitting up. Stones. Cold and clammy against her cheek. Was she in the dungeon? Had this been some kind of palace revolt? No. Mother ruled with an iron hand — surely it had been just an isolated incident. They must have stuffed her in some garderobe. Lurin shuddered. There must be a door, if only she could see.

She began to fill her lungs with air. If she exhaled the flame slowly she could see long enough to find the door.

At least they had not tied her up.

Princess Lurin saw the door on her first try. The flash of dragon's fire lit the space well. The problem was that she had to wait to draw in enough breath for a second try and then she was back in the dark. Still, she had seen enough to know that the tiny room was strangely shaped — not round — were there five or six short walls? It did not matter. She could feel her way to the door in the dark. She slid her hand along the smooth stones. At least there were no cobwebs. Indeed the stone she touched now felt smooth as polished glass. She paused, curious to look at it.

Softly she exhaled and as the flame licked at the stone she saw that it was glass. A mirror. It was framed in flame and instead of her own reflection it contained a deep swirling whirlpool of fire. That was all she had time to see before she was sucked into it and felt herself hurtling through space, choking with the acrid smell of sulphur.

She landed unceremoniously — and painfully. Perhaps if she had been used to flying through tunnels of flame she might have fared better. As it was she was bruised and singed and extremely annoyed. And once again in the dark.

Again, reluctantly this time she used her dragon's flame to see where she was. In the brief illumination she saw only that she was on the landing of a circular stone staircase but what it circled she could not tell. Obviously she had a choice of going up or down and one would be as good as the other, she supposed. She had seen a torch in a sconce on the wall not far away — she reached for it in the dark and was relieved to be able to feel it and lift it. Another blast of flame, and then she could stop using her dragon breath — her throat was raw and parched by now. But the torch did not light. Curses! It was burned out. She hurled it down the stairs, her temper a little appeased by the sound of it clanging and ricocheting off the walls as it fell down the narrow staircase. She would climb and see if there was some way out but first she flopped down to rest. Her throat was the main problem and she did not want to use her fire until she'd let it cool. She could bear to sit in the dark a little while.

CHAPTER ELEVEN

Queen Mariah had paused for only a moment to change on her way to the passage. She had met no one in the royal chambers but perhaps the search for Lurin had spread to other parts of the palace. It did not take her long to reach the transporting room but as she opened the door it was obvious that something was very wrong.

The tiny chamber still flickered and smoked and the sharp odor of recent use made her eyes water. Horrified, she stepped back into the tunnel. How could this be? She had not used the room since she had last visited the king. It was unthinkable that anyone could have discovered it, let alone learned the secret of firing the mirror. But it had obviously happened.

Mariah's anger would have been terrible to behold but since there was no one to vent it on, she controlled it. But she needed to be doing something. Action of any kind was better than sitting and waiting for the mirror tunnel to cool enough for use. She would have a long walk to fuel her fury. Whoever she found at the end of it would pay and pay dearly.

She covered a good distance of the passageway propelled by anger. Eventually she slowed, and began to realize her mistake. Better to go back and wait until she could use the fire mirror. She would use the time to plan. Someone or something had used the mirror passage. There could be only one answer. That wretched flying creature. She should have killed her when she had the chance. Everything had been going so well for so long. She had come here as a young woman, a novice, only beginning to experiment with her powers. She'd needed no potions or enchantment to trap the king into marrying her. Her remarkable beauty had been enough. Then in rapid succession she had borne three daughters. The king was handsome, sure of himself and besotted enough not to suspect that they were not his own. The people of the kingdom had rejoiced with him over the lovely young princesses. He was beloved by his people and they had accepted her as queen, awed by her beauty and apparent grace. She'd enjoyed that — the worshipful crowds that cheered below the balcony and bowed at her passing in processions with the king. There was power in that and she'd learned to love it. And had wanted more.

She moved swiftly, retracing her steps until at last she came to the tiny room. This had been one of the first of her triumphant spells. Finding this ancient passageway had been so lucky. It had given her access to the tower, a place already shunned as evil by the people of the kingdom, making it an ideal place for her to perfect her spells. Her work had gone so well there she sometimes felt she was being guided. And so her power had grown. So too had her power with the king. And for that she had used little magic. He had been delighted with his beautiful daughters, amazed by the incredible beauty of his wife and, like the people, in awe of her. He was by nature an obliging, easygoing man and she had found him easy to control. She'd allowed him his hunting and had flattered him by pretending to be unsure of herself as queen so that he felt she needed his support and advice.

Really — Mariah allowed herself a grim smile at the thought of it — he'd been so easily led, it was almost boring. Then, fourteen years ago he had defied her to meet the dragon and the flying girl. Her eyes flashed and her step quickened as she strode back down the passageway. Interference! Perhaps if the dragon had not been so inexperienced, or if they had come sooner, before she had gained so much control over the king's guards, things would have been different. The dragon had been quickly overcome — had even, in his death throes, turned on the king and that fool huntsman. The flying girl had been more of a problem. She had fled, disappeared after the battle. But her wounds had been terrible — no doubt she died.

Mariah flung open the door to the mirror chamber. Good! It had cooled and so had her anger. She was calm enough now to realize that it might be wise to have guards on hand in case she needed them at the tower. She could deal with the king herself, but a troop of trusted soldiers outside the tower might be useful if the dragon returned. And whoever had used the mirror passage would be waiting. She grasped the stone hidden in the folds of her cloak. It was the same one as that worn by Kenion, the captain of her guard. By the heat of it he would know to bring a few select men through the passage as well. Better! Now she was ready for whatever awaited her.

She gathered her cloak about her, held her torch to the mirror and was soon hurtling through the fiery tunnel.

She landed more gracefully that Lurin had before her. Much practise enabled her to calculate the time it took and her heavy black cloak protected her from the singeing her daughter had experienced. She stayed on her feet and arrived almost silently.

She reached for the torch immediately — knowing, even in the dark, exactly where her fingers would find it. To her annoyance she felt only the sconce that would have held it. Gone! Anger distracted her so that it took a few moments for her to realize that she was not alone. A rustling sound, a sharp intake of breath, gave that away.

Someone crouching motionless nearby. Was this the person who had used the tunnel? There was no doubt in Mariah's mind. Still, she knew she had the advantage, she could almost smell the fear, the paralysis that enveloped the unfortunate creature. Mariah felt no fear, only the sweet anticipation of vengeance.

And then an exhalation of breath and a blast of flame filled the stairway and wrapped her in it. Mariah saw nothing at first, then in the dying flame she could see that it was Lurin, flames licking her daughter's face, singeing her hair and gown. Lurin screamed, then rolled beneath the flames and down the stairs to safety.

Mariah heard the sharp crack as the princess' head struck the stones at the curve of the stairs and then there was silence.

The queen stood a moment until the flames about her subsided. How fortunate, she thought, she'd been wearing the fireproof cloak. Who would have thought that Lurin's dragon breath could be *that* effective. She would never have given it to her had she known the extent of the power. So it was Lurin who had used the tunnel. What else was the wretched girl plotting?

She ran a few steps down until she saw the crumpled body of her daughter and then, without checking to see if the princess was dead or alive, turned and ran silently up the steps. Who else was in on this? Lurin was not clever enough to have planned anything alone. Mariah recognized her daughter was beautiful and brave but definitely the least bright of the three girls. But she was easily influenced. Until now Mariah had thought hers was the only influence. Now it seemed the girl had somehow become involved in a plot to save the king. If so, who was behind it? The flying girl? She wondered if she would find the king gone or surrounded by allies when she arrived.

Queen Mariah stormed through the door as it slid silently open and was strangely surprised to find her unconscious husband lying alone. Indeed she was stopped by the fact that the room was as she had left it except for the death-like pallor of the man lying at her feet.

>─I─◇─O─◇─I─◄

"We are nearing the staircase now, I think," Talun announced.

Petaurus paused to catch his breath. "You said you thought it was deserted but you heard something?"

"I wasn't sure...it could have been the wind...perhaps an opening further up the stairs." His voice was hesitant.

"I think we should be prepared." He drew his sword.

"Perhaps I should go on ahead again? You could guard the girls," he added, more as a sign of respect than in expectation of the fighting abilities of an unarmed Petaurus.

Abruptly they came to the foot of the narrow staircase. The stone steps curved sharply upward. Room for one swordsman to defend it. Enough to give them time to flee. Petaurus nodded. "A sensible plan," he murmured as he leaned wearily against the wall.

Before Maighdlin could move forward to speak to him Talun had gone silently up the steps and out of sight. Mala found herself a dry space back near the turn in the tunnel and sat down to rest.

There was mutual concern as Maighdlin and Petaurus faced each other. She wanted to tell him that he should sit down to rest but she hid her worry. She knew it would hurt his dignity and she respected the strength, if not of his body, then of his will — the indomitable will that had brought him here on this long search for her.

"GranDa..." she began, not sure of what words she could find to say what she felt.

"Galea...." He spoke as if he had not heard her. For a moment he looked at her tenderly. "You have become a lovely young woman...." And then he seemed to be far away. "It seems such a short time you've been with us. I should have talked to you...confided in you...more about that time...the accident." He looked at her again. "But you were a baby...afterwards I did not want to burden your childhood with knowledge of ancient wrongs. Now I know it must be shared...I will not live much longer and you have a right to know...*must know*...." He smiled at her now, and there was some of his old teasing way in it, "...and knowledge is power, they say."

"GranDa?" He looked so tired, perhaps he should not be trying to talk. Before she could think of a way to put him at ease, he interrupted her again.

"Your mother knows some of it, but only what needed to be told at that time. For her own sake she was told no more." He lapsed into silence again. "The king knows, of course. But who knows what has become of him?" He glanced up the stairs. "...Or of what will become of us, now."

The stairs reminded her of Talun. Why had he not returned? And then she heard what she had dreaded. A startled cry echoed from the stairway above them. Before Petaurus could stop her she had slipped away and begun to climb.

The Princess Lurin's face was beautiful in repose. Maighdlin realized that she had never seen it other than contorted by anger or petulance. Now, lying on the stairs, lit by the flickering torch in Talun's hand, the princess looked pleasantly lovely. It took Maighdlin by surprise.

She'd come upon Talun as he stood over the princess only a moment before. "Did you...?" Though she didn't think he had — she'd had to do it for him last time.

"No...I found her lying like this."

Maighdlin bent over and touched Lurin's throat. There was a pulse but she was definitely out cold for the time being. Had someone brought her here still unconscious or had she been struck again? She could hear Petaurus voice calling from below them on the stairs.

"GranDa!" She looked at Talun. "I don't want him getting hurt!" If there was someone here knocking the princess out, then there could be fighting.

He nodded. "Keep him back if you can, I'll check." He handed her the torch, turned and moved silently up the dark stairway above them.

Maighdlin sighed impatiently. Talun was not a great one for farewells, was he? Who knew what lurked above them, or if she'd ever see him again. It would take GranDa a while to catch up. She might as well follow and see what

Talun might encounter. She could always duck back if there was trouble and have plenty of time to get back to GranDa.

Gathering her skirts she slipped quietly up the steps. She left the torch in a sconce nearby. It would not pay to draw attention by bringing the light with her.

CHAPTER TWELVE

———·———

Kour'el had left the other two standing below as she flew up to look in the window of the tower room that had so long been her prison. She had just had time to glimpse the dying figure of the king when the door slid open and the queen burst into the room. Luckily her attention was focussed on the moribund man on the floor: she did not glance up to the window and Kour'el was able to flutter silently out of sight.

So, we have found the king near death — and he is not alone. Stay and listen but do not interfere unless his life is threatened.

Kour'el could see Api'Naga and Geraint move back a short distance from the foot of the tower.

Do you think it would be possible for our friend here to squeeze through that window to help?

Kour'el knew it was hopeless. There had been barely room for her to fly through between the melted bars when she escaped. And she knew Api'Naga realized this too for he and Geraint began to circle the tower looking for some other way to gain entry. She wondered at this. Api'Naga had long ago told her there was no door but she did not have long to ponder on it for her attention was drawn to noise of movement inside and she dared to venture a look.

"So you still live?" Her shrill voice filled the chamber. "Wake up, then!"

There was no mistaking that grating voice even though she wore the old woman disguise. Kour'el shuddered, filled with pity for the helpless man below.

The king opened his eyes.

Since the queen was now bent over him Kour'el dared to move closer. Perhaps if he saw her hovering outside the window, it would give him some hope. She put her head through the window, resting her arms on the lumpy ledge. Being this close to her prison brought a wave of hopelessness, as if the confusion and despair she'd felt there had somehow lingered in the stones. She fought the feeling and was relieved to find it drowned out by the confusion of thoughts from the two people beneath her. The king's were fuzzy now, but she could sense his terrible thirst and weakness. How long had he lain in that state, she wondered? She had no doubt now that it had been he who had tried to summon the dragon.

But the thoughts that stormed her mind were those of the queen. She was not masking them now, thinking she was alone with the king, and her fury overwhelmed Kour'el. It was fortunate that she clung to the windowledge or she might have fallen. Again she struggled for control. She must remain and do what she could to help. Judging by the queen's plans now, the king was doomed and he was far too weak to resist her. Kour'el had not noticed the vial before. Her view had been blocked by the woman's body, and only now could she see the lethal amber liquid the queen held in her hand.

Queen Mariah paused and glanced toward the doorway. She did not recognize the young guard that stood there, sword drawn. Good. Her wily captain had sent someone dispensible. If he realized later that he had seen her poison the king, then his silence could be arranged. Dead men told no tales.

"Stop!"

Kour'el's voice was too soft to make much impact but the queen was startled nevertheless. Better still, the king's eyes opened. Yet even as hope leaped, it died. The king's eyes closed again in exhaustion.

"Don't drink! It is poison!" Kour'el tried again. Where was Api'Naga? She'd sent for him to come. Even if he could not enter the room his presence would help.

The guard was moving forward. And like the queen Kour'el first believed it was to protect Queen Mariah. Now Kour'el realized from *his* thoughts that he saw only an old woman and Kour'el's words had confirmed his own suspicions. His *king* was in danger. He raised his sword and dashed the vial from the woman's hands.

"What!" she screeched. "You *dare* attack your queen!"

The harsh voice reached Maighdlin in the passageway and stopped short her headlong search for Talun. Cautiously, she looked past the doorframe. To her horror, she saw Talun transfixed before the queen, whose arms were raised and whose angry face was terrible to behold. As Maighdlin watched, the queen drew a dagger from the black robe she wore and advanced.

"Talun! Move!" screamed Maighdlin, and ran forward.

"Petaurus! Can you go faster?" Mala begged. They were nearly at the top of the stairs now, but Mala could still hear the sound that had caused them to leave the moaning Princess Lurin at a run — or as near to a run as the old man could manage. A dozen marching guards, however well selected, do not move quietly between echoing stone walls.

The old man was leaning heavily on his walking stick, gasping for breath now but Mala knew there was nothing to do but keep moving. Whatever was ahead could be no worse than what was coming from behind them. Without a word she slipped under his arm supporting him as best she could and moving him on up the stairs. She only hoped that finding the princess would slow the guards a little.

There was light ahead. Petaurus gestured to her to blow out the candle he carried. She knew he could not have spared the breath to do that or to speak. Even before they could see anything they could hear a crash and then an angry voice that could belong to no one but the queen. Mala pitied whoever had inspired it for she had heard the queen in her rages before but nothing equaled what she was hearing now.

Then suddenly she understood. "Petaurus! It's Maighdlin!"

But the old man was no longer at her side. He had moved forward more quickly than she would have believed possible. Where had he got that reserve of energy? She rushed after him as he plunged through a doorway, and witnessed a chain of events that happened in a rush but which remained in her memory forever frozen in a single, wondrous tableau.

There was the queen, a dagger upraised in her hand, but not aimed toward Talun, who was caught as if by a spell; the dagger was meant for the emaciated figure on the floor whom Petaurus was crouched beside, his staff raised and ready to strike. But more wondrous still was the figure of a girl, a winged girl, her face framed by wonderful wild hair, who hovered above the queen. No wonder Talun was in shock.

But now Maighdlin had rushed from Talun's side to her grandfather's, and Mala saw the dagger come down, straight toward her friend's breast. "Maighdlin!" she screamed.

Petaurus saw it too, and in a voice full of agony cried, "No, Galea!"

Recognition crossed the winged girl's face as she repeated the name in a strange sing-song voice, "Galea!".

And then everything was moving again — so fast that Mala could not keep up. There was a blur as the flying girl swept down and seized Maighdlin, lifting her out of the dagger's way, though later they would find the tear in her dress where the blade had nearly entered her breast.

Talun, like a statue come to life at last, rushed to Petaurus' rescue, the old man crumpled across the body of his king as if shielding it with his own body.

But Talun's sword struck at thin air for the queen was gone. Vanished? Not quite. She was behind Mala now, screaming for the guards who now emerged from the stairway. Above them all, Maighdlin kicked and struggled to escape the grasp of the flying girl. And then there was a roar such as none had ever heard — and the roof above them began to melt.

The queen's guards stopped in their tracks and the flying girl swooped down, pushing Mala into a safer place with Maighdlin beside her, away from the molten metal that cascaded down the wall until there was a hole large enough to see the sky. Through that hole came the body of a man and the head of a dragon.

The man landed moving surprisingly quickly for someone of his bulk. Before anyone had time to recover he had seized the guard nearest Talun and taken his sword. The others remained as if frozen, staring up at the dragon. And then the queen stepped into the doorway, a terrible smile on her face.

"So dragon, you test me again!"

She was gloating in triumph but she stayed where she was, with her guard shielding her from Talun and the flying girl, and everyone else in the room between her and the dragon.

"There are guards behind me, a regiment outside on the ground. If you try to attack, all in the room will die and you will be doing me a great favor. We will tell the people of the terrible dragon who attacked and killed the king and..." she waved her hand dismissively around the room and her voice dripped vitriol, "...these *loyal* subjects... and I will be the rightful queen and heir to the kingdom, not just the consort of a useless monarch!."

There was silence then. Maighdlin and Mala joined hands. They were doomed if the dragon attacked and doomed if it went away, for how long could Talun and the man beside him — brave though they might be — resist the queen's guards?

Then came a voice weakened by pain. "You can...not...be heir to this kingdom." There was movement and the soft fluttering of wings as the flying girl crossed the room which seemed to give the king energy for his voice now was strong and sure. "You cannot be heir to the throne because *I ruled only until the rightful heir might come of age!*"

The shocked hesitation of the queen's guards gave Talun and the other man just enough time to seize the queen and place her as a shield between the king and the swords of her men.

The tower is indeed surrounded, and the bowmen are preparing to shoot at the roof, Api'Naga sent.

Kour'el knew she must act quickly. Until a short time ago she would have tried to save the king: but now there was the young girl across the room, the one whose name — Galea — she'd been given by the Great One all that time ago. The vessel spoken of was neither a ship nor a cup. It was that young girl. Her body contained the bloodline, the rightful heritage to rule this land.

— Should I? she sent to Api'Naga. There was no time for his response. Kour'el swooped forward, arms extended. But then someone was pushing past the guards in the hallway. A disheveled but strikingly beautiful young woman shoved her way angrily into the room giving the guards the sharp edge of her tongue as she did so. She stopped at the doorway obviously shocked.

"Mother!" She rushed forward as if to attack the two men. "Let go of her at once...I...." And then she stopped and began to gasp for breath.

"No!" Mariah shrieked.

She snapped free of the men, leaving them holding nothing but the heavy cloak, and rushed toward the girl to stop her. It was a fatal mistake. The blast of flame enveloped the queen; there was a flash of lightning that filled the room and then nothing but the smell of sulphur remained. The body of the queen lay on the stone floor, burnt and crumbling, wisps of smoke the only movement.

Chapter Thirteen

Shock and bewilderment filled the room again. Kour'el almost smiled at the tortured thoughts of the captain of the Queen's Guard as he tried to decide with whom he should throw in his lot and loyalty. He had never liked the headstrong young princess and she lacked her mother's intelligence for manipulating and planning. He doubted that she would listen to his advice. Thus he dropped to one knee in homage to King Vassill, signaling his men to follow suit.

Kour'el lifted the king but the poor man's efforts to speak went unheard until Api'Naga flew down into the room and sent the thought of silence to everyone there — though Kour'el wondered whether it was that or merely the presence of the dragon that silenced them.

When the flying girl moved the king, Maighdlin saw her grandfather slump aside, and she realized that Petaurus was injured. So everyone else listened to the king's story of the baby who'd been brought by the flying girl and the dragon so many years ago, a child he would have brought to the palace but for his grievous injuries, while that child, now grown, gathered her grandfather in her arms.

"GranDa!" If only she could wake him. Everything was all right now. The queen was gone, the king still lived. "GranDa...please wake up..."

And then he opened his eyes and smiled at her. "I'm not really your GranDa," he said weakly, "but it's been wonderful to have you acting as if I were...and it was good for my daughter too, to have you after her own baby died." He paused, gasping for breath, and Maighdlin did not like the rattle in his chest that the effort caused. But he smiled again in the old way and she was comforted. "...And Bron has had a wonderful sister..." For a moment his voice was strong again.

He looked up at Kour'el, hovering above, then back at Maighdlin. "The one who brought you saved me, and though I could not heal her injuries, I hid her until she died. Then I built a funeral pyre deep in the forest where the dragon died, and the queen never knew that the flying one had lived long enough to show me where you were hidden." He sighed. "It was so long ago, and now it has been accomplished." His voice was low, straining to speak, "...And I am proud of you...and you will be a...good... queen."

Then the rattle was louder, and then it stopped and he slumped back in her arms. It was only then that Maighdlin saw the blood on his clothing and found the wound on his chest where the queen's dagger still lay buried.

Behind her she could hear the voice of the king introducing her as the rightful queen and she was dimly aware of people in the room bowing. But it all seemed a dream. What was real was that GranDa was gone. And Maighdlin could only sit and hold him and weep.

>-+-+>-0-<+-+-<

Queen Galea stood in heavy robes and crown on the royal balcony and waved to the crowd below. Above her the

248

amethyst crystals of the palace sparkled in the sun. She smiled not because she was happy but because the people expected it of her and she was grateful for their joy, though she herself felt nothing but sorrow.

She tried to keep her eyes on the crowd below but from here she could just see over the walls of the city to the countryside beyond and to the blue mountain that crowned the horizon. It had been a simple, happy life, and now it was gone forever. Even if she could stop being queen and go back to being just Maighdlin again there would be a great emptiness because Gran'Da was gone. Her eyes filled with tears, blurring the distant mountain and the cheering crowd below.

Before he died, King Vassill had arranged her succession and had helped her reorganize certain things about the palace. Everyone that Queen Mariah had appointed had been replaced. Thanks to Marika and and her connection to the palace grapevine, people loyal to the king — and now herself — had been found and promoted to positions they had only heard of before.

Marika, now married and standing just inside the doors of the royal chambers as close to Brede as she could get, and Mala were First Ladies-in-Waiting to the queen. And Maighdlin's mother — foster mother — had been given the title of Duchess of Blue Mountain by King Vassill himself before he died. That made Bron a lord, though it didn't seem to have changed him any except for his clothing. Maighdlin — Galea — could see him out of the corner of her eye ducking out from behind their mother waving to her from just inside the balcony door. That brought a smile too and she straightened her shoulders under the heavy purple and ermine robes. She would work hard to make the land a joyful place again for all the people and for children like Bron to grow up and be happy.

Tautarus, although not well enough to serve as Captain of the Queen's Guard, had been made advisor to Talun, who now held that position.

"If this were one of the magic tales we learned as children," Mala had teased as she'd struggled to arrange Maighdlin's coronation robes, "we would discover Talun to be the prince of a faraway land who was here in disguise looking to wed a noble princess...like you!"

Maighdlin had laughed then for the first time since the terrible events in the tower. "...Or a goose girl...like you!" she replied, hugging her friend gratefully.

The whereabouts of the other two princesses was still not known. Perhaps they had been swept back to the place Mariah had first come from — Maighdlin hoped so. But there was the possibility that they had merely gone into hiding and would reappear to lead Mariah's courtiers against the new queen.

As for Princess Lurin she'd been taken into far exile by the dragon Api'Naga.

To everyone's amazement the dragon had grown to an enormous size after spending a night in the courtyard of statues like himself. The gardener who worked there had reported the mysterious disappearance of one of them. "But it was broken anyway, your Majesty," he told Maighdlin. Queen Galea had suggested that he plant flame trees in its place.

The sound of a laughing song seemed to cascade through the air above her and she looked up to see a girl swoop and dive on wings as diaphanous as gossamer, her wild hair shooting sparks as she flew. The joy of Kour'el's flight song lightened Maighdlin's heavy heart. She was grateful that the bird-girl and the dragon had agreed to stay on for a while before they returned to their own country.

Maighdlin almost lost her crown as she strained her head to look to the battlements above her. Yes, there was the noble head looking over edge of the turret above her. Now a flash of flame from the mighty dragon stilled the crowd, and the cannons began their salute.